Dusty Boots

Dusty Boots

Major Mitchell
&
Jerry Mitchell

Shalako Press
Oakdale, CA

DUSTY BOOTS

For information contact: Shalako Press P.O. Box 371, Oakdale, CA 95361-0371 http://www.majormitchell.net

ISBN: 978-0-9964235-6-4

Cover Artist: Jinger Heaston
Cover format: Karen Borrelli

Editor: Judith Mitchell

PRINTED IN THE UNITED STATES OF AMERICA

ACKNOWLDGMENTS

This book is a combined effort of many people. We would like to thank Kelly Phillips, Josie Costa, Pat Decker Nipper, and the several other people who read the manuscript, caught the authors' mistakes, and offered their input.

A big thanks to author Stephen Lodge for the cover photograph.

Most of all, hugs and kisses to Major's wife and partner, Judy, whose editing turned our scribbles into something readable.

DEDICATION

This book is dedicated to fans of the old west who keep the tradition alive.

Dusty Boots

"Yeah, I see him," Rob Mayfield said as the yellow dog barked. He had been watching as the rider guided the tan mustang toward the house at a slow trot. Small clouds of dust gathered as each hoof dropped, and swirled upward to cling to the rider's boots and pant-legs. East Texas was dry the summer of 1884.

The dog continued his barking and tail-wagging as the rider came to a halt at the gate. "If you was any kind of watchdog, you'd bite his leg off, instead of acting like a fool."

"Now, what kind of a greeting is that to give your big brother?" the short, stocky man drawled, and slid to the ground. "Hi, Buster. How're you doing, boy?" He ruffled the dog's ears.

"The kind of a greeting that says you shoulda been here, Bill. You knew she was sick. You didn't even come to the funeral."

"Yeah, I knew she was sick, but I didn't know about her dying until a week ago. Then, I came as soon as I could."

"What do you mean, you didn't know. I wrote that very morning and took the letter to the post office myself. Then, I hung around until it left on the train an hour later." Rob turned as if he were leaving, but spun back to yell.

"We waited two days to bury her, hoping you'd show up! You know what that means? Two days in this heat? We waited as long as we could. It's only fifteen…maybe sixteen miles from Douglass to Clarksville. It ain't that far. I've ridden it myself in less than a day."

"Yeah, that's true." Billy paused, brushing the dust from his shirtsleeves to study his brother. "But I don't work for old man Taylor anymore. I haven't been in Clarksville for more'n a year."

"You don't? Where've you been, if you don't live in Clarksville?"

"Oh," Bill took a handkerchief from his hip pocket and began wiping the dust from his boots, "your letter caught up with me in Wichita."

"Wichita? Wichita Falls?"

"Uh-huh." Billy nodded.

"In Kansas?"

"No, dummy," Billy said with a laugh. "Wichita Falls, Texas."

"What the heck were you doing in Wichita?" Rob took the reins of his brother's horse and led it toward the watering trough.

"Seeing the world, little brother. Not too much," he warned as Rob let the horse drink. "He's pretty hot."

"I don't call a trip to Wichita seeing the world."

"Neither do I," Billy said with a laugh. "That was the forwarding address I gave when I left Clarksville, and I just happened back through there when I got your letter about Mama dying."

"Where've you been besides Wichita?"

"All over. I've been to Arkansas, and Louisiana. Do you know," he came closer as he stuffed the handkerchief back in his pocket, "they've got the prettiest women down there, with the darkest eyes and hair black as coal? They speak French."

"Yeah, I know," Rob said with a nod. "They're called Cajun."

"That's right. Where'd you learn that?"

"I read it in a book, Bill. I didn't quit school and go

running around like you." Rob tied the horse to the picket fence and walked toward the old house with a rocker sitting on the porch.

"Gate needs fixin'," Bill said as the bottom hinge popped free, causing the gate to flop awkwardly.

"A lot of things need fixing, but I've only got one of me. I've been busy plowing the field, tending the stock and taking care of Mama. I even took a job at the livery in order to pay the bills. You wasn't here."

"I'm here now, little brother."

"Yeah, so you are. Might as well grab your stuff and come inside…now that you're here."

"Yeah, I'm here." Billy Mayfield heaved a sigh as he studied the place. It had been a little over three years since he rode away, vowing never to return. The whitewash on the fence and house had disappeared, exposing gray weathered boards, warped by the sun. The small lawn and garden that his mother had been so proud of was nothing but dust and weeds, making Billy wonder if it wouldn't be better to remove the fence all together. He paused on the porch to stare at the field.

"I only plowed ten acres this year and most of it is burnt off, 'cause we didn't get any rain," Rob said as if he were reading his brother's thoughts. "Here." He shoved a cup of coffee toward Bill. "It might be kinda strong. I made it earlier."

"Can't be any worse than some of the camp coffee I've drank. Thanks," he added, toasting his brother and taking a sip. "Did you bury her next to Pa?" Bill took a second sip and set the cup on the porch railing.

"That's where she wanted to be."

"Well, maybe she's happy now. God knows I couldn't please her."

"Aw, come on, Bill. You didn't even try," Rob said with a smirk. "All she ever wanted was for you to stick around and do your chores, but you was always running off and getting into some sort of trouble."

"Yeah, I did my share of that." He laughed. "But I suppose you've done better." He took another sip of coffee and stepped off the porch and into the yard. "This place is worse than I left it, Rob."

"I tried. That's more'n I can say for you," Rob yelled, as he followed his brother into the yard. "I was still in school and working at the livery. Then, I'd come home and work the field and care for the animals. I didn't have much time for fixing what needed fixing, 'cause, my big brother wasn't anywhere around."

"So, you've told me. The point is, little brother, it ain't that easy, is it?" Bill tossed the remnants of his cup as he continued. "This place is cursed, Rob. Take a good look at it. I mean, a real good look. Forty acres of dust, rocks and weeds."

"It wasn't always that way. When Pa was alive…"

"That's right," Bill said, cutting his brother off. "When Pa was alive. Now, you sound just like Ma. She always said that whenever I complained, or suggested that we sell the farm and move into town. But the thing is, Pa's dead, Rob, and he's been dead nearly ten years. He ain't coming back.

"This place is cursed. Just look at it." Billy waved his arm in a wide arc. "It killed Pa when you were what…six years old? Now, it's killed Ma, and it'll kill you too, if you hang around here much longer."

"Is that why you left?" Rob snickered. "You thought there was a curse on this farm?"

"You bet. And I just didn't leave, Rob. I ran as fast as my horse could take me, and I didn't stop until I reached Clarksville. Since then, I've been to dozens of other places."

"When you should've been back here helping Mama."

4

"Yeah, right, and turn out like you." Bill laughed as Rob glared at him. "Look at yourself, little brother. You're an old man at sixteen. All sour and dried up like your cotton field. This farm has sucked the life out of you. You ought to sell it and come with me."

"And go where?"

"Where? Anywhere you want. Where would you like to go, little brother?" He chuckled as Rob continued to glare. "It's a big world out there. And with the money you'd get from selling this place, you could go anywhere you wanted and do whatever you wanted. I could take you to New Orleans on a train. You've never been on a train, have you?" He waited until Rob shook his head.

"I have. You might even find yourself a Cajun gal and get the blood moving inside those dried-up veins of yours. And eat? They can throw some stuff together that'll burn your tonsils out, and have you begging for more. You haven't been to a party until you've been to one of their wingdings. They've got some fiddlers that'll make any we've got in Douglass sound like they've got two busted hands."

"Sell the place? You're asking me to sell Ma's house?" Rob backed away. "You go away and come back three years later, after she's dead, telling me to sell her home? She loved this place, Billy."

"Yeah, she sure did that, didn't she? Look," Bill placed a hand on Rob's shoulder, "all I'm saying is, think about it. Ma's happy now. She's with Pa, and he's happy 'cause he's got a chance to plow some good cotton fields up in heaven. That's all he really loved. Breaking the ground and watching things grow. Well, he's got that now, and she's with him. Let them be, little brother. They're not here, and your hanging onto this place isn't going to help. It'll kill you, just like it did the both of them."

"But, selling the place...I don't know, Billy."

"All I'm asking is to think about it. Like I said, it's a big world, and there's a whole lot more than Douglass, Texas to see. Now, come on," Bill said, slapping Rob on the shoulder. "I think it's time I unsaddled Jake and got myself cleaned up. Maybe we can go into town later. I'll tell you what, let's both get cleaned up, and I'll buy you a steak. Is that redhead still waiting tables at Maud's Place?"

"She's married, Billy."

"Married? When's something like that ever stopped me?" Billy Mayfield laughed as he led his horse toward the barn.

Chapter 2

Rob had to admit that his brother did clean up pretty nice. Billy Mayfield might have been an inch shorter than Rob's six-foot frame, but he packed more weight and muscle, and had their father's dark hair, complexion and good looks. Rob, on the other hand, had always been tall and skinny, with mouse-brown hair and freckles. He had also, for as long as he could remember, envied his brother's way with words. Even as a child, Billy could talk his way out of getting a licking, while Rob's best attempts only made things worse. Rob sat chewing a bite of tough steak, realizing his brother hadn't lost an ounce of his charm.

"What'd you want to go get married for, Zora? You knew I was coming back for you."

"Coming back? Why, Billy Mayfield, I believe that's the biggest lie you've ever told." Zora Whitefield's scolding was tempered by a smile and a sideways glance from her green eyes.

"Lie? I came right into this restaurant and stood right over there by the counter," he pointed, "and told you I'd be back as soon as I made something out of myself. Ain't that so, little brother?"

Rob pretended to choke on the steak as the pretty redhead glanced at him.

"Well, you're no help."

"Rob's not a liar like you are, Billy Mayfield. Why, I ought to wash your mouth out with soap for telling such fibs." Zora turned with a swish of her hips and retreated to the safety of the counter.

"Ya know," Billy leaned across the table with a grin, "I think she's even prettier than when I left. Lord, I've gotta have me some more of that."

"I'm telling you, she's married Bill. Better leave her alone."

"Or what?"

"Or what?" Rob did choke this time, and paused to cough. "Geez, Bill. She's got a husband. That's what!"

"Henry? Henry Whitefield?" Bill leaned back in his chair laughing. Then he glanced to see if Zora had overheard their conversation, before leaning closer and lowering his voice.

"I used to beat Hank up nearly every day after school, just to keep myself in shape. He'd get so scared seeing me coming, he'd pee his britches. What's he gonna do?"

"He runs the general store and sells guns, that's what. He ain't a little boy, and it might be different now."

"You've been stuck on that farm too long, little brother." Bill leaned back and toasted Rob with his coffee. "People don't change. A coward's still a coward, no matter how old he gets."

"Maybe," Rob nodded, "but not when it comes to a man's family."

"Think so? Hank's like this town…it never changes. It's the same as when I left three years ago, and it'll be the same a hundred years from now."

"I've got news for you, big brother. They've got plans for making some changes around here. They're even thinking of renaming it, and calling it *Avery*."

"Avery? After Ed Avery," Billy asked with a snort.

"Yeah, why not? He was one of the founding fathers, and the first station attendant for the railroad."

"Ed Avery's the *only* station attendant Douglass has had. But, geez," Billy laughed, "what's Ed think about it?

That's like having your name plastered on a chicken coop. Some honor that'd be."

They grew silent as Zora approached their table with a coffee pot.

"Can I get you boys something else," she asked as she refilled Bill's cup. "Maybe some apple pie?"

"Now, where'd you get apples this time of year?" Billy laid his hand casually across her left wrist as she leaned to refill his brother's cup. She didn't remove it.

"Maud uses dried apples, just like everyone does. A world traveler like you should know that, Bill Mayfield."

"Apple pie might be nice. But what I'd really like, is for you to forgive me, Zora. I really did come back to take you with me." Bill slid his hand to caress hers as he talked.

"My husband might have something to say about that. I'll get your pie." Rob cringed as she smiled at his brother.

"What'd I tell you?" Billy leaned close to whisper as Zora swished her way to the counter and cut the pie. "She's still got the old fire burning."

"My God, Bill. You're gonna get yourself shot, if you're not careful," Rob hissed.

"That ain't likely. Hank ain't got the guts to brace me in a gunfight. Besides, even if he did, I could out-pull him in my sleep any day of the week, same as I used to whip him. What I am gonna get is…" he grew silent as Zora returned with two large pieces of pie.

Rob took small bites of apple pie, and thoughtfully sipped his coffee as his brother continued wooing the pretty waitress. *That ain't right, Billy. Henry Whitefield won't like you talking to his wife this way. Better let her be.*

Chapter 3

"Where're you heading?" Rob paused at his task of drying the supper dishes when his brother came from the bedroom adjusting a string tie.

"There's a poker game going in the back room at the cotton gin." Bill paused to look in the hall mirror and make a final adjustment, then smooth down an unruly hair with his palm.

"Isn't that game reserved for rich farmers and cattlemen like Jake Bradford?"

"Little brother," Bill laid a hand on Rob's shoulder and laughed, "there isn't a rich farmer or cattleman in Douglass. Jake might have a little more than most around here, but he certainly isn't rich. Beside, I've got money. Certainly enough for this game." Bill grabbed his hat and paused at the door.

"Wish me luck, little brother."

"Yeah, good luck with your game." The door closed, and Rob watched through the window as Bill mounted the tan horse and rode toward town. He shook his head and finished stacking the dishes.

There had been a lot of talk concerning Billy that Rob didn't care for. Of course gossip always traveled fast, especially in a community as small as Douglass, with only forty-eight folks including himself, to do the talking. They were saying that Billy was shiftless and lazy, and called him a loud-mouth braggart that drank too much. Rob refused to argue against the rumors, using the Christian upbringing his mother had taught as an excuse. The truth was, he knew the rumors to be mostly true.

In the past three weeks, he'd only seen his brother occasionally, and that mostly over the suppers Rob cooked. Then, Billy would excuse himself and head into town. Folks were also talking about his philandering with a married woman. It wasn't hard to place a face and a name with that rumor. Rob had always been on friendly terms with Henry Whitefield, but the man refused to look at him the last time he enter the store, much less speak to him. Rob simply laid what he thought was the correct change for a sack of flour and bag of coffee on the counter and left. The fact that Billy was sporting Zora Whitefield was well-known, and no one tried to hide or even whisper their suspicions. The only question in anyone's mind was when would Henry do something about it?

The gossip angered Rob, not so much for what they were saying, but because, like it or not, Billy was his brother. They had the same parents, had grown up, played, ate, fished, argued, fought and laughed for as long as he could remember. Now that he was back, little as he had seen of his brother, some of that feeling had returned. It was good having him home.

Perhaps Billy was right, Rob reasoned as he hung the frying pan on the hook above the wood-burning stove. Maybe he should sell the place, then they could leave Douglass and he could see some of the places Billy talked about. That'd also get him away from Zora before something bad happened. Their leaving would also stop the gossip, and their parents could rest in peace. Jake Bradford had mentioned his buying their farm the day of Mama's funeral. Rob decided he would talk to him first thing in the morning.

Chapter 4

"Sure, I thought about buying your place." Jake Bradford sat his lanky frame on an empty crate in front of his cotton barn and rolled a cigarette. "It borders up next to mine, and might be a better piece of ground, given the proper conditions."

"Such as?" Billy asked. Rob had asked his older brother to come, thinking is was only proper for him to be present while selling the family farm.

"Rain, for one thing. Your ground sets a little higher, and gets dryer without rain. I'm gonna lose my shirt during this drought, but as hard as Rob's tried working his field, he won't be able to harvest nothing but dust."

"You mean, you don't want to buy our farm anymore, Mr. Bradford," Rob asked.

"Didn't say that." He struck a match and touched it to the cigarette.

"Then, what are you trying to say," Billy said with a snicker.

"I'm saying I don't know if I could afford it," Bradford snapped back. "Especially after the way you picked everyone's billfolds with your fancy card playing last night."

"You calling me a cheat?" Billy laughed louder than needed, something he used to do before getting into a fight at school, and Rob clamped his fingers around Billy's wrist.

"No," Bradford glanced toward Billy's guns without a sign of emotion, "but some are. I kinda figure anyone stupid enough to sit in a game and lose as much as I did doesn't have any right to complain. All I'm saying is, I'm

12

broke…cleaned out, and I don't know how I'm gonna make it if I don't get some sort of crop this year, which isn't likely."

"Okay," Billy said and jerked his hand free. "How much you figure our place is worth to the right buyer?"

"Oh, that depends."

"On what?"

"On a lot of things, boy. It'll be worth a lot more in a good year, with plenty of rain and a nice crop. But right now, you're going to play hob finding a buyer that'd give you more than twenty five or thirty dollars an acre. Besides, that's something you'd better discuss with the bank. Your ma borrowed quite a bit of money against the place a year or so before she died."

"That true?" Billy jerked around to stare at his brother.

"Well, yeah, I guess so."

"Whatta ya mean, you guess so?"

"I knew she borrowed some money, but I don't know how much. I thought she paid it back," Rob said with a shrug.

"Fact is, she didn't," Bradford said, crushing the cigarette butt under his heel. "Another fact is, she owed a lot of people money, including me."

"Why were you interested in buying the place then, if she owed you money?" Billy crinkled his brow and gave the man a crooked grin.

"'Cause I happened to like your folks, and thought it'd be nice to do something for their youngest son. I considered buying the farm and allowing Rob to stay in the house and work for me. Maybe, when this drought broke, and he got a little older and learned some things, he might even buy it back. That is, if he was interested."

"But you're not making the same offer to me? That right?"

"No, Bill, I'm not making the same offer to you," Bradford said, laughing and shaking his head. "Besides, you wouldn't stay and work the land if I did. You certainly wouldn't pay back the money she borrowed from the bank, or other folks she owed. No, you'd take the money and be gone quicker than a piece of fried chicken at a church social."

"You got that right. I never did cotton to that farm or the town of Douglass, for that matter," Billy snickered.

"No one's arguing with you, boy." Bradford turned toward Rob and asked, "What are your plans now, son?"

"I don't know. A lot depends on Billy. I guess I'll tag along and go where he goes."

"I hope not." Bradford grabbed the empty crate he'd been sitting on, and tossed it onto a stack of empty crates near the barn door.

"And what's that supposed to mean," Billy said. The grin had vanished.

"It means," the lanky man turned to glare, "that you're full of yourself, thinking you can do most anything and get away with it. And if your brother goes tagging along, you're going to get the both of you into trouble. No, Rob," he shook his head, "if I was you, I'd stick around Douglass and find work and stay away from your brother. As hard as things are here, they aren't nothing compared to what it's like inside a prison."

Chapter 5

"Thirty-five dollars!" Bill Mayfield stared at the small pile of money and laughed loudly. "Fourteen years on that farm, working their fingers to the bone, and that's all it's worth? Thirty five dollars?" They were seated inside Stanley Weston's office at The Bank Of Oak Grove, while the banker tried explaining the equity value of the Mayfield family farm.

"No, that's not quite true," Stanley said, tapping the stack of papers with his finger, "that's the value after deducting what your mother owed."

"Thirty-five dollars?" Bill repeated.

"Yes, thirty-five dollars. Do the math yourself. And, that might be generous."

"What's that supposed to mean," Billy said, wiping his eyes on a shirtsleeve. He couldn't seem to quit laughing.

"What it means is," Stanley Weston leaned across his desk to glare at Billy, "that there's nothing funny about it…there may be some money owed to private people I don't know about. I was only concerned about what Mrs. Mayfield borrowed from the bank and several businesses."

"Businesses? What businesses?" Billy's laughter and loud voice caused the teller to poke his head through the door to see if everything was okay.

"Yes, businesses. Your mother bought most of her groceries on credit. She also owed a large sum for cotton seed, horseshoeing, doctor bills," the banker lifted the stack of papers and let them fall, "and these are only the ones I know about. As I said, I'm positive she might have borrowed money from people that I'm not aware of. Given the current market value of your farm, including the house and barn…which needs some repair…and deducting what's owed," he tapped the papers, "the Mayfield farm is worth thirty-five dollars. You can sign the papers and take the money, or not, that's up to you. But I hope you don't."

"And why not," Billy said, stuffing the money into Rob's pocket.

"It means, the bank doesn't want your farm. I'll have to spend a lot of time trying to sell the place in order to recoup our losses. But since you've taken the money, I guess the farm belongs to us. Sign here." He dipped a pen in the inkwell and held it toward Bill, who signed with a grunt and passed it toward Rob.

"Thank you Mr. Weston," Rob said, shaking the banker's hand.

"You're welcome, Rob. Any idea what you are going to do now?"

"No," Rob said and shook his head. "Find a job somewhere, I guess."

"Well, good luck son." Stanley Weston watched the brothers leave before collecting the papers on his desk and stuffing them into a filing cabinet. "You'll need it."

Chapter 6

Rob spent the next week packing and giving things away. He had no idea how parting with his mother's personal possessions would make him feel, and was shocked to find himself sitting on the back porch crying, as Freda Thompson left with the rocking chair and Buster, the Labrador, in her wagon.

"Hell, it's just an old broken-down chair." Billy snorted. "I've sat in better in nearly every hotel I've been in."

"It was Mama's chair, Bill, and Buster and I grew up together."

"Yeah, I liked that dog too." He laid a hand on Rob's shoulder and softened his voice. "But he's getting old and we can't take him with us, now can we? Just like most of the stuff in this house. And that's another thing." He crossed the living room toward a pile of belongings Rob had stacked in a corner. "I hate to say it, but you've got way too much stuff packed. Get rid of some of it."

"Get rid of it? I can't, Billy. That's all I've got…everything I own."

"And how do you plan on taking it?"

"I don't know. I suppose…"

"Well you supposed wrong. We're taking horses, Rob, not a wagon train. We're only taking what we can carry in saddle bags. Ya got room for a couple of changes of clothes, ammo, a little grub and a few personal things. Whatever you can stuff in a saddle bag and nothing else. Got

17

it?"

"What about everything else?"

"We'll have to give it away or burn it."

"Burn it," Rob yelled. "Burn Mom and Dad's things? What's the matter with you? That's all they had. It'd be like burning them!"

"Yeah, maybe you're right. But, let me tell you something, little brother. Mom and Dad aren't here now, are they? They're both dead, and we can't be taking all their belongings where we're going. So, you've got two days to decide what to do with it, 'cause I'm leaving, with you, or without you. You decide." He pointed a finger toward Rob's nose.

"Thing is," Bill paused as he grabbed his hat and dusted the rim, "we don't own the place anymore, and that includes the furnishings...such as they are. Ma's old rocker you just gave away actually belonged to the bank. I don't see as how we've got much choice. See you later."

"Where're you going," Rob asked as Billy opened the door.

"Got ta say my goodbyes to a woman, Rob. Something a young boy like you wouldn't understand." He grinned and studied his reflection in the only mirror left hanging. Black hat, vest, gloves, belt and shiny boots. Even the shirt he was wearing had black vertical striping. The pearl grips on the matching pistols and the silver spurs were complimented by silver conchos on his gunbelt and hatband, reminding Rob of a drawing he once saw on the cover of a ten-cent novel.

"Zora Whitefield?"

"What do you think, little brother?" Bill laughed.

"You're gonna get yourself shot, messing around with another man's wife. That's what I think."

"Not likely. See you around," Bill said, and bounded off the porch, leaving the door open.

Yeah, Rob nodded thoughtfully as he watched his brother climb on his horse and disappear toward town. *I can see what Zora Whitefield might see in you.* Billy Mayfield did pose a striking figure. *Trouble is, you stand out in any crowd. It ain't hard to spot you, big brother.* The way folks turned to stare as they entered town together, or walked down the street, made Rob uncomfortable. They'd never done that when he was by himself, only when Billy was present. Not that they had been unfriendly toward Rob. On the contrary, everyone seemed to like Rob Mayfield. They treated him as someone who belonged...something comfortable, someone you might not notice, but would certainly miss it he wasn't there.

On the other hand, it was different with Billy. Billy Mayfield demanded attention, and got it. His loud, boisterous voice, infectious laughter and to-hell-with-the-world attitude caused people to notice him. Rob could remember cringing with embarrassment as a child while his brother caused many a ruckus in church. He later admitted it was only because he thought the sermons were too long and boring. Besides, Rob thought, it was another way for Billy to get noticed.

Yes, people certainly notice you. Rob returned to his sorting, trying to figure what might fit into a saddlebag. The trouble was, he had never owned a saddlebag. *Let's hope those fancy clothes don't make you a better target for Henry to shoot at. I'd hate to see blood all over that shirt you've got on.*

Chapter 7

He didn't see Billy the rest of the evening, or the next morning. After fixing himself a breakfast of fried eggs, bacon and a bowl of grits, Rob decided he had better ride into town and see about buying a set of saddlebags with the thirty-five dollars he had gotten from the sale of the farm. He found several people standing outside Whitefield's General Store, waiting to get in.

"What's the matter with Henry? He sick or something," Rob asked, as he joined the others in their quest to enter the store.

"Something, would be my guess," Ed Avery, the rail station attendant growled.

"Humm," one of the women huffed and looked away.

"Perhaps you'd better ask that brother of yours. You might find out," Clara Womack hissed.

"I ain't seen my brother since yesterday."

"That's no wonder," the first woman said.

"Well, whatever's keeping him had better hurry. I've got the ten-thirty arriving in fifteen minutes," Ed said, checking his gold pocket watch.

Rob had resigned himself to waiting like the others when he heard his brother's voice from the corner of the building. "Pssst. Hey Rob. Come here a minute."

"Huh?" Rob stared at Billy's grinning visage poking around the corner as the women turned their backs and looked the other way.

"I said, come here."

"Okay, what do you want?" Rob rounded the corner to see his brother trying to pull his boots on. His shirt was unbuttoned, with an uncombed shock of hair poking from underneath the black hat.

"Get my horse." Bill pulled the last boot on with a grunt and began stuffing his shirttail inside his britches.

"Your horse?"

"Yeah, it's at the livery. Hurry!"

"Billy, what's going on?"

"Not now, Rob. Get my horse. I'll tell you later. Hurry now!"

"Okay, as long as you tell me what's going on."

"I will. Now, get the horse."

Rob crossed the street and walked toward the livery at a fast pace. He had never seen his brother look so disheveled, unless it was when he first woke up when they were children. One thing for sure, he had never seen Billy more excited, unless it was when he was caught spooning with the parson's daughter in the peach orchard. Sherman's Army couldn't have caused more of a ruckus than what happened that night. Priscilla was crying and begging her father not do whatever she was afraid he might, while Mama gave Billy the what-for. Bill, on the other hand, just grinned and giggled like he had a bellyful of wiggly worms tickling his insides. Rob had failed to fully appreciate the situation, until Jake Bradford explained what had happened.

Priscilla had since married Chester Brown, a man nearly twenty years older than her. They had eighty acres of cotton south of town. Rob paused cinching the saddle, wondering. *Na*, he shook his head and continued tightening the cinches. Priscilla had two children and had put on some thirty pounds since the peach orchard. Knowing his brother, there wasn't any way Bill would give her a second notice. He was halfway from the livery to the store, leading the horse, when a woman screamed.

"Stop him! Please, somebody stop him!"

"Jesus!" Rob stopped in the middle of the street as Zora Whitefield passed him, clad in her nightgown with her red hair streaming in the breeze. Twenty yards or so ahead was Henry, armed with a double-barreled shotgun. Rob started forward at a run, but stopped as his brother came from behind the store.

"Oh, good Lord," he said as he was knocked to the ground and almost run over by the horse. "Here, wait." He grabbed the reigns and pulled the horse to one side, out of the line of fire.

"Hold on, Hank. Don't do nothing foolish. It ain't worth it," Billy said, holding his left hand in the air.

"Ain't worth it? You bastard!" The angry storekeeper aimed the shotgun, and was instantly pitched backward into the street by the report from the gun in Billy's right hand. Billy ran forward to point the pistol at Henry's head as Zora stood in the middle of the street screaming.

"No, you don't," he said as the storekeeper moaned and reached for the shotgun. Billy tossed the gun toward Jake Bradford's feet as the man approached. "I warned you not to try, Hank. You couldn't whip me with your fists when we were kids, and there's no way you can beat me in a gunfight."

"I think you've caused enough trouble. You'd better leave town," Jake Bradford was saying as Rob led the horse to where they stood.

"I plan on doing just that, Jake. In fact, that's what I was fixing to do when Hank decided to give me a bellyful of buckshot. Ain't that right," Billy said, and laughed as he nudged the wounded man with the toe of his boot. Rob handed the reigns to his brother as he stared at the prostrate storekeeper. He had a wound just below his left collar bone that was bleeding profusely. He couldn't remember seeing his brother draw the gun, but couldn't remember seeing one in his hand prior to the shooting either. All he knew was, his brother had shot a man who had a shotgun pointed at him, before he could pull the trigger.

Rob was once again brushed aside as Zora burst through the crowd and cast her disheveled body across her husband, crying.

"I'd make it fast, if I were you, and don't come back," Jake Bradford growled.

"Don't worry," Billy said, and mounted the horse in one fluid motion. "We won't be coming back this way. Will we, Rob?"

Rob glanced at the angry faces of those gathered in the street for the first time, and knew the Mayfield welcome had been revoked.

"No, I don't guess we will." He looked at Jake Bradford and added, "I'm sorry."

"Me too, Rob. Me too." The big man turned and began barking orders as Rob walked toward his horse, repeating the words inside his head. *"Me too, Rob. Me too."*

Chapter 8

"That ain't the way I heard it happened." The crusty-looking cowhand with a week's worth of stubble leaned against the bar and grinned.

"No?" Billy Mayfield set his glass of whiskey on the table and twisted in his chair to stare at him. The other four men seated at the poker table moved away like dancers on cue.

"Not according to what I heard."

Bill had been retelling the story of his gunfight with Henry Whitefield in the streets of Douglass and as usual, was adding his personal embellishment to the story, when the stranger began to refute his claim. Rob had listened several times a day since arriving in Cookville, as Billy retold the incident to anyone who would listen. The tale seemed to grow larger with each telling, but this was the first time anyone had disputed Billy's version. Rob paused his sweeping to watch as Billy grabbed his drink and ambled over to where the cowboy stood. He took a casual sip and leaned against the bar.

"Then suppose you tell us how it happened."

"What I heered was, that you was poking the storekeeper's wife, and he found out about it."

"Well, I've never denied that," Billy said with a laugh. "She was the prettiest woman in town. Hell, she was the *only* pretty woman in town. And, everyone in town knew about it before he had the guts to say anything. Go on." He took another sip and stared at the man.

"They said he asked you to leave her alone, but you just laughed and kept right on messin' around with her."

"True, true. But you see, she seemed to want me just as much as I wanted her. Now that makes for an interesting combination."

By now, Billy had nearly everyone inside the tiny *Trail Dust Saloon* laughing. Everyone except the cowboy, who took another swig of beer and wiped his mouth with the back of his hand.

"I heered her husband caught you two in bed the morning it all come down."

"Well, yeah, I'm not denying that either. She *was* pretty."

"Yeah, but I just heered you say that when the storekeeper came at you with that shotgun, you drew and fired before he had a chance to pull the trigger. Ain't that so?"

"That's what I said, and I was there."

"Well, a feller named Jake Bradford says you already had your gun drawn when you come around the corner of the building and pulled down on the storekeeper. So, which is it?"

"I don't see as it makes any difference," Billy said and took another sip. "Hank Whitefield had a double barreled twelve gauge pointed at me. I shot him before he pulled the trigger. That's a fact."

"Maybe so," the cowboy said with a snicker. "The difference is, the man was defending his honor, and you already had your iron pulled when he come at you. You ain't nearly as fast as you think you are, pup."

He had no more than gotten the words out, when Billy tossed the remainder of his drink in the man's face, and cracked him over the head with his gun.

"Is that fast enough for you? Stupid ass," he said as the unconscious cowboy slumped to the floor. Billy holstered his pistol and returned to his chair. "Now, where were we," he said, picking up the hand he had been playing.

"Not, so fast."

Everyone in the saloon turned as Sheriff Hocking pushed his way inside and allowed the batwing doors to swing freely as he walked toward the table. He was a large man in his fifties, with a graying moustache and a business-like manner.

"I want you out of town. Now!"

"Why, what's wrong sheriff," Billy said with an air of innocence.

"What's wrong? I just watched you give that man a concussion, and you ask what's wrong? You've been hanging around here all week, drinking and bragging how fast you are with guns and women. Sooner or later someone's gonna take you serious, and one of you is gonna wind up getting killed. Worse yet, you've been pestering women all over town, and several of them are married. One of their husbands might get lucky and put a bullet in you, then I'd have to lock one of my own citizens up.

"Your brother's got a job and hasn't caused any problems, so he can stay, if he wants. But, you're going," Sheriff Hocking said with a nod.

"Well, I haven't done anything but sit here, minding my own business and playing cards," Billy said with a snicker as he studied the cards in his hand.

"Don't try woolin' me around, boy. I'll take that fancy gun away and bend it over your head. Get up from the table and out the door...now!"

"Okay, okay," Billy said and raised his hands as the sheriff drew and cocked his pistol. "Take it easy. We're going. Just let me collect my money."

"Leave it. Get going." Hocking motioned with the gun.

"That's my money," Billy said.

"Not anymore. That's payment for your being a nuisance, and patching your friend on the floor back together. Now, out the door before I lose patience."

"Alright, I'm going." Billy paused at the door to stare at his brother. "You coming?"

"Like I said, he ain't done anything but work and keep his nose clean," Hocking said. "He's welcome to stay, if he wants."

"He's my brother," Billy yelled. "Rob, you coming or not?"

"Yeah," Rob nodded as he removed the apron, "I'm coming."

"That jacksnipe's gonna get hisself kilt, shore as spit," said an old man by the door as Billy stormed outside.

"I just hope he doesn't get his brother killed in the process," Sheriff Hocking added as Rob followed.

Chapter 9

"How much money have you got," asked Billy as he reined his horse to a halt. The two men were on the outskirts of Harvard Switch in the bottomlands of the Big Cypress Creek. The smell of fresh-baked cornbread, wood smoke and roasting pork filled their nostrils. It was getting late and time for supper.

"About twenty-five dollars," Rob said, checking his pockets. "You?"

"Nothing," Billy said, as he started his horse forward at a slow walk.

"Nothing? I gave you most of the money we got for the farm. What happened to that," Rob asked. A dog on the porch of a weathered shack started barking, and he fought to hold his horse in check while several black children poked their heads through the door to stare.

"That was only thirty five dollars, if you remember," Billy said with a snicker. "You kept the money we got for the animals, which was a site more. What happened to that?"

"You borrowed it, remember?" Rob looked down as his stomach growled. The smell of food was getting stronger.

"Oh, yeah." Billy laughed. "I had a bad run at the poker table."

"You're always having a bad run of luck, Billy."

"Our luck's bound to change little brother," Billy said.

They walked their horses down a wide roadway that seemed to follow the St. Louis Southwestern Railway.

Scattered houses dotted the opposite side road, away from the train tracks. Rob could see the rail switching house and what looked like a cotton gin a few hundred yards ahead, at the opposite end of town. A heavy set black woman was busy sweeping the porch in front of a ramshackle store front, and looked up as the two men stopped.

"Excuse me, Ma'am," Billy said, scooting his hat to the back of his head and giving the woman one of his best smiles. "I don't see a restaurant or boarding house anywhere. Could you tell me where we might get us something to eat? My brother and I haven't eaten all day. We've got some money and can pay."

"Yes sir," the woman said after a long minute. "What you is smelling is the barbecue they're having at the Methodist church. If you was to sit through one of Pastor Armstrong's sermons, and toss some money into the offering plate, I'm shore the folks will feed you. I plans on going there myself after I finishes here.

"As to where you're gonna spend the night, I got no idea," she added as she continued with her sweeping. "Ain't no hotel or boarding house 'round here. Ain't no need for one. Train just comes and picks up cotton, then goes. No one ever gets off or goes anywhere that I know of, and I knows just about everything that goes on around this place. You two is the first white boys I seen in awhile, except for them that drives the train. You is certainly the first ones that's come traipsing into town big as brass asking for a place to stop and eat. You have to excuse folks if they stare."

"Thank you, Ma'am," Bill said, touching the brim of his hat. "Lucille Woods," she said without looking up.

"I beg your pardon?" Billy stopped his horse as it started forward.

"Folks calls me Lucy, but my full Christian name is Lucille Woods."

"Well, thank you for the information, Lucy. It was

nice meeting you." Billy touched the brim of his hat again and urged his horse forward.

"Ma'am." Rob tipped his hat. "I hope to see you at church." He trotted his horse after his brother as the woman continued her attack against the Texas dust.

******

"Oh, Lord," Billy mumbled over a mouthful of barbequed pork rib. He took another greedy bite and continued talking as he chewed. "This...is the best...pork ribs...I think I've eaten."

"Well, I sees you boys found the church okay." Lucille Woods paused at the log where Rob and Billy were seated and gave them a huge grin. She had two plates piled high with ribs, beans, turnip greens and cornbread.

"Ma'am," Rob said, vacating his spot on the log. The action caused the several people seated around to cease their eating and conversation and stare.

The expression of shock on Lucille's face vanished after a minute and she smiled. "No, Sir. You just sits right there and enjoy your ribs. I gots to take this here plate over yonder to my lazy husband. He figures I still gots to wait on him, after I work like a slave and he don't do nothing but whittle wood and talk."

"Yes, Ma'am. Enjoy your meal," Rob said.

"You shore is cute, yes sir. Enjoy your ribs." She wove her way through the crowd laughing, as Rob sat down.

"What'd you do that for?" Billy leaned close and hissed the words

"What?"

"Offering her you seat, you numbskull."

"'Cause she's a woman, Billy."

"No she ain't." Billy leaned closer to Rob's ear and continued talking in a hushed voice. "She's a nigra. White folks don't give up their seats for a nigra. You know that."

"I don't care what she is, she's still a woman, and a nice one at that."

"Well, suit yourself." Billy took another bite of rib. "But…," he mumbled as he chewed, "you caused everyone to stare. These folks ain't used to being treated that way."

"Well, maybe it's time someone did treat 'em that way." Rob sopped the turnip juice in his plate with corn bread and stuffed it in his mouth.

"Ain't gonna happen. Besides, it embarrasses them." Billy shoved a spoonful of beans in his mouth and continued talking.

"And another thing. There wasn't any need of putting a whole five dollars in that offering plate."

"Why not? It was a good sermon, and you're eating their food," Rob said. "Besides, it would've nearly cost that much to eat at Maud's Place back in Douglass."

"Yeah, but we're short on money. A dollar would've been more'n enough." Their argument was cut short as the pastor wove his way to their log and squatted on his heels.

"I don't think we've been properly introduced. I'm Pastor Ezra Armstrong," he said, extending a hand. "It's shore nice to have you boys come and visit."

Rob wiped his palm on his pants and shook the man's hand. "Hi, I'm Rob Mayfield. This is my brother, Billy."

"Sorry," Billy held up a greasy palm and grinned.

"That's quite alright. The ribs are kind of messy, and I wouldn't want to see you wiping your hands on those nice clothes of yours. I'll see if one of the women has a rag you can use."

"Thanks, I'd appreciate that. By the way," Billy said, licking his fingers, "these are the best ribs I've eaten, and I've been to some pretty fancy places, including New Orleans."

"I see," Pastor Armstrong said with a nod. "I'm sure Ivory will be happy to hear you said that."

"Is he the big fellow doing the cooking," Rob asked.

"Yes, folks call him Hard Ivory. He was the first one into these bottomlands and built a house. The railroad made him section foreman when they came through, and lots of other folks started coming and setting down roots and growing cotton. Ivory's done pretty well for himself, and treats folks right. He went and built a steam cotton gin, so folks don't have to ship their cotton someplace else and get cheated by city folk."

"He's sure a big man," Rob said thoughtfully, studying the rippling muscles in the man's arms and back as he moved around the fire pit.

"Oh, he's shore enough that," Pastor Armstrong said with a laugh. "Some claim Ivory's most of six-foot six-inches tall and two-hundred-sixty pounds. I don't know if that's true or not, but he's shore enough a big man. He don't take to no nonsense either. You treat Mr. Ivory with respect, or you pays the consequences."

"Who's that pretty girl," Billy asked and pointed with his fork.

"Mmm-umm," Pastor Armstrong said and shook his head after spying the smiling girl seated at a table. Rob had to admit to himself the young lady was indeed beautiful, perhaps one of the prettiest girls he had seen.

"That's Wilma Ivory," Pastor Armstrong was saying.

"I can see the devil's done put the fires of lust into your loins, but you stay clear of that girl. You hear me, boy? That's Hard Ivory's daughter, and she might look older, but she's only fifteen. And Ivory don't cotton to men trying to spoon around Wilma."

"Why? I think she likes me. What would happen if I did," Billy said with a laugh.

"Listen to the man and leave her alone, Bill," Rob snapped.

"I never said I wouldn't. I'm just askin', that's all."

Billy sniggered.

"What would happen? There's a reason folks call him *Hard* Ivory, son. Last man that went spooning after Wilma almost met his maker. Ivory busted Theodore's jaw, and laid his head open with an ax handle. Mmmm-umm," Pastor Armstrong shook his head, "I thought we lost him for sure. And he was a black man. No telling what Ivory might do if a white boy made after his little girl. Ivory still ain't forgotten he was a slave before the war, and he don't cotton to too many white folks. Since then, he's fought Comanches, tornadoes, and all kinds of wild animals." The pastor stood and stretched his back.

"Well, I've got to go see how some of my church folk are doing, before they decides to get themselves another preacher." He paused to point a finger at Billy.

"You best remember what I said, boy, and put that fire out inside your loins. Wilma Ivory has got the wanderlust, but you stay clear of her if you want to see tomorrow."

******

They decided to bed under a large cypress in the church yard, and leave early the next morning. Rob was exhausted and fell asleep within minutes of his head hitting the saddlebag he chose as a pillow. He was awakened around two o'clock by what he mistook as the bellowing of an angry bull. Then he heard a girl scream as a man cried out in pain. He rolled over to wake Billy, but his brother was not there. "Oh, Jesus," he said, running in his sock feet toward the commotion, "please help me."

Chapter 10

Rob rounded the corner toward the rear of the church in time to see a giant smash a meaty right hand into Billy's ribcage. The blow caused his brother to fold with a cry of pain.

"No, please don't!" Rob threw himself between the two men, only to be knocked backward. He lay in the dust, unable to move, and listening to shouts and commotion caused by stamping feet. It wasn't until someone had kicked dirt into his open mouth that he was able to roll to his hands and knees, coughing.

"You alright, boy?

"Huh?" He stared into the concerned face of Lucille Woods.

"I asked if you was alright. So, is you?"

"I reckon." Rob glanced toward his brother crumpled on the ground. He was nude from the waist down. Six grown men, counting Pastor Armstrong, were holding Hard Ivory as the angry man fought against their grip and shouted.

"You don't look alright," Lucille was saying.

"I ran between them, trying to stop him from killing Billy."

"That was a dumb thing to do. Got yourself a bloody nose in the process," she said, wiping Rob's face with her apron. "Could also get yourself killed getting in Ivory's way when he's angry. Don't wanna go doing things like that."

"He's my brother. Is he…?" Rob started to crawl toward Billy, but Lucille's grip on his arm held him fast.

"Lucky to be alive, that boy is." She continued wiping at his face. "Here, hold your head back so I can stop this bleeding. There's lots of good folks looking after your no-count brother, and he's gonna be okay. Lord only knows why. Someone fool enough to go messin' 'round Ivory's daughter, after he's been told not to, deserves what he gets."

Rob allowed his eyes to drift toward the tear-streaked face of Wilma Ivory. The girl was crouched against the church wall, trying to cover her nude body with her rumpled dress. Two women tossed a blanket around her shoulders and led her away as he watched.

"I don't know why Ivory's so set on trying to protect her anyways," Lucille was saying. "She's about as no-count as that brother of yours. She don't like living here a'tall, and has tried running off several times. Fact is, the devil done put the fires of lust into that girl's veins long ago, and nothing her daddy, Pastor Armstrong, or even her mama says is gonna put them out. He ought to just let her go and be done with it.

"There," she said standing, "I think the bleeding's stopped. I like you boy. I don't know what happened to that brother of yours, but your mama raised you right. You got manners and good common sense about you. But, you'd better take your brother and git before Ivory finishes the job."

"I'm afraid Lucille's right son," Reverend Armstrong said, helping Rob to his feet. "Ivory caught your brother and Wilma in the very act, and it ain't over by a long shot. He'll kill your brother if he sees him again. You'd best leave tonight."

Rob stared as two men helped Billy to his feet and led him toward the front of the church. He was hunched over and holding his ribs with both hands.

"Is he able to ride?"

"That don't matter none, now does it," Lucille said,

brushing some of the dust from Rob's shirt. "You had best get him on that horse and git. He's shore gonna die if Ivory sees him in the morning."

"Some of the folks are saddling your horses right now," Pastor Armstrong said, grabbing Rob by the arm. "Come on now," he pulled Rob forward, "we're gonna help you get him on the horse, then you git. Understand me, boy? You're gonna git, 'cause I don't wanna hold no funeral for a white boy that ain't got the sense God gave a jackrabbit."

"Yes, sir. I understand." Rob watched as the two men helped Billy up on his horse in his long johns, then tossed his trousers across the saddle in front of him. Billy leaned hunched forward moaning. A third man handed Rob Billy's gunbelt.

"Here, I reckon these guns belong to your brother. You'd best be keeping them 'til you gets down the road a piece."

"Yeah, thanks," Rob said. He slung the belt across the pommel of his saddle before shaking the pastor's hand. "Thank you sir, for everything. I'm sorry about what happened."

"Thank you son, but it weren't none of your doing. You're welcome to come visit anytime, but your brother had best stay away, if he knows what's good for him."

Rob took the reins and nudged his horse forward. He could hear Lucille Woods talking to Pastor Armstrong as he led Billy's bay at a slow walk toward the road.

"Those two boys are shore different. Makes one wonder if they really got the same mother."

"One thing's for certain," Ezra Armstrong said with a chuckle. "They fell on opposite sides of the fence when they was born."

Chapter 11

"What's the matter with you? You must've known what was going to happen. The preacher told you to keep away from that girl. He even told you that her dad almost killed the last man he caught her with. You almost got us both killed!" Rob's angry voice caused a flock of sparrows to flee the tree they were camped under. He had kept the horses moving at a gentle walk until early dawn, then stopped in a grove of trees. He estimated they were still only six, maybe eight miles south of Harvard, and Hard Ivory.

"Na, you were safe enough. It was me that big bastard was after," Billy said with a groan.

"Really? I guess that's why I got this blood all over my shirt. Huh?"

"You got that 'cause you were stupid enough to think you could stop a train with your face. You had a gun. Why didn't you shoot him?"

"Shoot him? Why…what…" Rob's voice rose to a squeaky pitch.

"Yeah, you should have shot him. It might've saved us both from getting a beating," Billy said.

"It might have gotten us hung. What's the matter with you, Bill?"

"Nothing's the matter with me. The matter's with you? First of all, they don't hang white people in Texas for killing a nigra."

"No? For your information, *big brother*, we were in a black town. Everyone there has dark skin, and that *train* you accused me of trying to stop was the man who built the town. I think they might've hung us for killing their founding father, and who would know? Besides," Rob paused to shake his saddle blanket and stretch out under the tree, "it wouldn't feel right to shoot a man who's trying to protect his daughter."

"Protect her?" Billy gave a snort. "Make her a slave is more like it. She told me herself that gorilla won't let a man get anywhere near her. She even begged me to slip her out of town and take her away. I might've, except she's black. I didn't want to be stuck with a nigger hanging around when we got to a large town."

Rob raised up on one elbow to stare at his brother. "Why'd you go sparking her behind the church if you didn't want to be seen with her, then?"

"Why? Oh, God!" Billy held his ribcage laughing. "Ah...oh Lord that hurts. Don't make me laugh. Why'd I meet her behind the church? If you don't know that, little brother, you've got a lot to learn."

"Maybe," Rob said laying back and closing his eyes. "But not if it's the kind of stuff that keeps getting us into trouble. Do you realize," he sprang back to a sitting position to glare, "that we've been run out of three towns because of you and women."

"Wrong, little brother. We've been run out of two because of women. We were run out of Cookville because the sheriff saw me whack that big lunk in the head."

"There was a woman in Cookville also. I saw you with her."

"There was more'n one woman, but we didn't get run off because of them. You've got a lot to learn about life in general, especially women."

"Not if it means treating women the way you do, Billy."

"And what's the matter with the way I treat women?

You tell me what."

"Well, for one thing, you use them and run off leaving them miserable and crying. Take Zora for instance. She was a happily married woman until you came along. You caused her to commit adultery, Billy. You know what that means? Folks will be talking about her and saying things from now on. Then, you even shot her husband. Now you tell me, is that anyway to treat a woman? I don't think so." Rob lay back and closed his eyes.

"As far as Zora Whitefield is concerned, she wasn't happily married when I came along, or she wouldn't have gone to bed with me. We were lovers long before she married Hank. Way back before I left home. And as far as Wilma Ivory goes, she came looking for me. I heard what that preacher said, and I saw her daddy and hell yes, he scared the dickens out of me. But she wanted me, so who was I to tell her no?"

"You should've told her no. Look at you now, all busted up. Almost got yourself killed. Think she was worth it?"

"Oh, yeah. She was worth it," Billy said with a chuckle.

"What? I don't believe you." Rob sat back up to stare.

"I've never been with a woman who made love like her, Rob. I might've taken her with us, if she'd been white."

"Good God! What have I gotten myself into?" Rob lay back and covered his face with his hat as his brother laughed, then jerked the hat back off. "Mama didn't raise us that way, Billy. Remember? She took you to Sunday School and we said our prayers every night. Didn't any of that stick with you?"

"Yeah, we went to church every Sunday and listened to boring sermons. And yeah, we prayed every night and what good did it do?"

"What good did it do?" Rob shook his head in disbelief.

"Yeah, what good did it do? Mom and Dad prayed...oh boy did they know how to pray. And all they ever got for their prayers was that little shack they called home and a lot of hard work on a dirt farm. They worked themselves to death for nothing. You got that Rob? Nothing! Well, not me, little brother. That's why I left home. I saw them dying one day at a time, little by little, and getting nothing in return. So, I said to hell with it and got out while I still could."

"So, you left God and everything that Ma taught, just like the farm. Is that it?"

Billy stared at Rob a long minute before answering. "Yeah, I guess you could say that. All their god did was kill them...torture them in the hot cotton fields until they died. I wasn't sticking around for him to do it to me also."

"I feel sorry for you, Bill." Rob covered his eyes with his hat.

"You'll change your tune," Billy said with a chuckle, and grabbed his ribs with a grimace.

"I doubt it."

"Oh, you will the first time a pretty girl gets you into bed. Let me tell you, little brother, that's the real heaven. Not the stories you heard about in Sunday School."

"You're sick! You know that? Real sick." Rob rolled over as his brother laughed.

Chapter 12

Theodore Russell paused to glance at the two men before hanging the cotton sack on the scales.

"Who do you reckon they are, Ted," Theodore's wife asked as she drug her full sack toward the scales. Hildegarde would have normally been at the house preparing a noonday meal for the workers, but due to a financial crisis in the Russell farm budget, Theodore had not been able to borrow money from the bank to pay seasonal workers. The woman had risen in the wee hours of the morning to prepare breakfast, and sandwiches that could be eaten cold with canned fruit from the root cellar at noontime. Ted could not remember hearing her complain about the hard work around the farm once in the twenty years they had been married, and eyed his wife with pride before answering.

"Don't know, Hildie, but you'd better hang around. Looks like one of 'em's hurt, by the way he's hunched over."

"Probably ett something that's sitting wrong in his stomach," she said, wiping her brow. "Might see a lot of that, if this heat keeps up."

"Heat's tough on them that's got to work out in it alright, but better'n what the rain would bring if we don't get the cotton picked." Ted marked the weight of his sack in the log book before climbing up the side of the wagon and dumping a storm of white fluffy balls inside.

"I take that back," his wife said, still watching as the riders drew closer.

"Take what back?" Ted dropped to the ground with a

thud and hung his wife's sack on the scales.

"About that boy with the fancy duds. He ain't sick in the stomach. Someone's beat the stuffins outa him."

"Really?" Ted marked the weight of his wife's sack in the book and climbed back up the railing to dump her load.

"Yes, really," she said, as the riders came to a halt in front of the wagon waiting to receive the cotton. "And it looks like he's busted up pretty good."

Ted dropped back to the ground as one of the riders removed his hat.

"Ma'am," he said with a nod. "My name is Rob Mayfield, and this here is my brother, Billy. As you can tell, he's kind of in a bad way. I was wondering if there is a doctor anywhere that can take a look at him? I don't have any money to pay him with, but I'm willing to work, if that's possible."

"Whoever gave him the licking did a right good job," Ted said, taking a closer look at Billy. "What happened?"

"He got into it with a man back in Harvard called Hard Ivory."

"He got into a fight with Ivory and lived? Either your brother's tough, or just plain lucky," Ted said with a laugh.

"Stupid's more like it," Rob said, shaking his head. "Is there a doctor I can take him to? I think he's all busted up inside."

"What's the matter, Ma?"

"Got a boy here that's been in a fight." Hildegarde glanced sideways at the girl dragging a loaded cotton sack toward the scales. She was short and petite, with long blond hair poking from under her bonnet. The faded sundress she wore was dirt-stained and soaked with perspiration, and her bare feet kicked little clouds of dust as she hoisted the neck of the sack toward the scales.

"You listening, boy?"

"Ma'am?"

Hildegarde grinned as the boy snapped his attention back toward her. He had been watching her daughter, Clara, intently. "I said the closest doctor is in Pittsburg, almost five miles away. How is he for traveling?"

"I don't think he'll make it that far," Rob said with a shake of his head.

"Didn't think so. Clara," she said turning toward the girl. "We'd best take Mr. Mayfield and his brother to the house and see what we can do. You make a pallet on the back porch with the blankets in the cellar. I'll come along and see what we can do for his brother. I might have to run and fetch the doctor, as poorly as he looks. That is, if it's alright with your father," she added with a glance at her husband.

"I reckon you'll do what needs to be done. Don't know what's gonna happen to the cotton if it rains. Anyone stupid enough to get in a fist fight with Ivory should be left to his own devices," the man said with a growl.

"I'll come back and work for you after I see about Billy," Rob said.

"You know anything about cotton, boy?" Ted eyed him up and down.

"That's all he knows," Billy Mayfield said with a chuckle, then grimaced with pain.

"Got some busted ribs, don't ya boy? Lucky you still got your head. Okay," Theodore Russell said with a nod. "You go see about your brother, then come back and I'll see what you know about cotton."

"Yes Sir," Rob said as the big man turned away mumbling. "I'll be back as soon as I can."

"Well, don't just stand there." The girl grabbed the reins of Bill's horse. "We have work to do, and you're taking up time." She led the horse toward the house at a brisk walk as her mother kept pace and held onto Billy.

"Yes Ma'am," Rob said, trailing his horse behind.

"Don't *yes ma'am* me. My name's Clara Russell. And if you want to impress my father, you'll get out into the field as soon as you can and work your fool head off."

"Why would I want to impress your father," Rob said with a snort. He picked up his pace in order to walk next to the girl.

"I don't know. You were bragging about how much you know about cotton. I thought you might be trying to impress someone." She walked even faster.

"I didn't say I knew anything about cotton. That was my brother. But, as a matter of fact, I *do* know something about cotton. My parents owned a farm near Douglass. I grew up there."

"Well, we'll see what you know when you get in the field, won't we?"

"I reckon."

Hildegarde shook her head as Clara and the boy eyed each other and laughed. It was the first time her daughter had shown any interest in a boy, and she had picked a stranger with a beat-up brother in fancy clothes. *Oh well*, she sighed. Clara was fifteen, and it was time for such things.

The house was a large rambling affair with a screened-in porch and unpainted, weathered siding. Clara led Billy's horse to the rear and held the screen door open.

"Better help Ma get him inside. I'll get some blankets from the cellar."

"Yes, Ma'am...I mean Clara," Rob added as she scowled. Her sunburned nose had a generous sprinkling of freckles. Billy moaned, and gasped with pain as Rob and Hildegarde helped him from the horse and onto the porch.

"Wait Clara," Hildegarde said as her daughter started for the cellar. "Better let me have them guns you've got on," she said, with a nod toward Billy. "There ain't nothing for you to shoot, and the condition you're in, you'd probably shoot your foot off. Besides, I've got a little boy that likes looking at such things. We keep what guns we've got locked in a closet."

Rob unbuckled the belt and passed it onto Clara's extended hand without even glancing at her mother. "Thank you, for everything."

"You're quite welcome," she said with a smile. Her white teeth and blue eyes sparkled as she turned away. "I'll lock these up and be right back with the blankets."

"Her full name is Clara Jean Russell, and she's fifteen," Hildegarde said as she helped Billy into a crude homemade chair.

"Ma'am?" Rob rushed to help her.

"I just thought you might be asking, so I told you. I don't know anything about you or your brother, but I can smell trouble brewing. I just don't want my daughter caught in the middle. Understand me?"

"Yes, Ma'am. There won't be any trouble as far as your daughter is concerned, at least not from me. Billy's the one that causes that kind of trouble, but I don't think he'll be doing that for awhile either."

"Figures."

"I'm sixteen."

"Say again?" Hildegarde stared at the boy.

"I said I'm sixteen. I thought you might like to know."

******

Clara bounced up the steps with an armful of blankets as Hildegard began unbuttoning Billy's ruffled shirt.

"Make him a pallet over there," she pointed, "next to the wall. It'll block some of the wind and afternoon sun. And you," she turned to Billy, "had best hold still while I have a look-see. Say," she said as she pulled back the shirt to reveal a bruised ribcage, "he did a number on you, didn't he?

Reckon that hurts, doesn't it," Hildegard said as Billy reacted to her pushing and poking on his side. "Ted was right about your busted ribs. I'll fetch the doctor, but I don't think he'll do anymore than wrap you up and tell you to behave yourself." She straightened herself with a sigh.

"Best fetch him a pitcher of water and one of them sandwiches, Clara, then get back to the field. I'll be gone most of what's left of the day, and your pa's gonna be fit to be tied." She paused to eye Billy up and down.

"Having you under foot wasn't something we really needed. We got us a decent crop for the first time in years, but no money to hire workers. So, it's been just me and my husband and three young'uns. But, I guess we'll make do. We always have."

Clara disappeared into the house and returned with a pitcher of water and a plate holding two ham sandwiches and canned apples.

"Here, you boys eat this when you get hungry. I've got to go back to work."

"I'm coming with you," Rob said, shoving his hat down on his head.

"One of those hunks of ham are yours." She motioned toward the plates on the floor.

"It'll keep. Your pa's cotton won't if it rains, and I don't like the looks of those clouds in the east. We'd best get going."

Hildegard Russell watched as the young couple walked briskly toward the field. The boy seemed nice enough, but she had a bad feeling about his brother lying on the pallet...if he was indeed his brother. One could never tell about such things. *Yes*, she thought, *every living creature has its mating season.* She just hoped her daughter had enough sense to choose the right one. She heaved another sigh before heading toward the barn to fetch the horse and buggy.

Chapter 13

"You did a man-sized job this afternoon, and I'm much obliged." Rob glanced up as Theodore lit his pipe and took a seat next to him on the steps. He had found a cool place on the rear porch to watch the last of the pink disappear in the Texas sky as stars began to twinkle. The smell of fried potatoes and cornbread drifted through the open window as Hildegard and Clara prepared supper. Clara's younger brother, Peter, was feeding the chickens, while her older brother, Lloyd, milked their three cows. The Russell farm was a vast improvement over the one Rob had grown up on. Better land, house, animals and cotton crop. His mother would have loved it.

"Thanks. But as I said, I ain't got any money, and I won't be staying and eating your food without earning me and my brother's keep. I reckon I'll have to work off whatever your wife paid the doctor, also." Rob finished by heaving a sigh.

"I can appreciate that. I was brought up the same way." Theodore drew deeply on the pipe and blew a cloud of smoke into the air as the two sat in silence. The man next to him used the same tobacco his father had smoked. Rob closed his eyes, allowing the memories to sweep across him with the cool evening breeze, until Clara poked her head through the back door and yelled.

"Ma says supper's ready, and y'all better get yourselves in here before she feeds it to the dogs!"

"Guess we'd better get washed up and to the table,"

Theodore said, slapping Rob on the back. "She means it."

Rob paused to stare at Billy lying on the pallet.

"Don't pay him no never mind, boy." Theodore chuckled as he poured water into the washbasin by the screen door. "He's taken enough laudanum to sleep a week. Probably the best thing for him. What'd he do to get Ivory so riled? Start messing with that daughter of his?

"Figures," he said when Rob shrugged his shoulders. "He's not the first white man that's gone after her. How about you? You try sporting her?"

"No, sir!" Rob shook his head.

"No, didn't think you would," Theodore said, studying Rob closely. "You got more sense, and that's a good thing. Ivory's got himself a mighty fine looking girl, but he ain't gonna cotton to her tangling with any white man a'tall. Besides, you like the land too much to be thinking about things like that. Don't you boy?"

"Yes, sir. Reckon I do."

"Yes, sir," Theodore said with a nod of agreement, "I could tell by watching you this afternoon. No one works the cotton like you unless he's got a farmer's heart." He finished scrubbing his hands and arms and grabbed the towel hanging on a wooden peg.

"Better scrub them paws of yours, or Hildie will send you right back out here, if you show up with dirt under your nails.

"Yes, sir," he continued as Rob grabbed the lye soap and dunked his hands into the milky water, "that's a good thing, being a farmer. Ain't but three things that's gonna last and amount to a hill of beans when a man's finished. His religion, his family, and the land. Those will be around long after he's been planted. Remember that, boy. Now," he slapped Rob on the shoulder and passed him the towel, "let's go get some vittles."

Chapter 14

"You like it here, don't you?"

It was more of a statement than a question, and Rob glanced at the girl on the opposite side of the row. Her bonnet-covered head bobbed up and down as she picked the white fluffy bolls clinging to the bush. He waited a long minute before answering.

"Yeah, guess I do. Why?"

"No reason. I just noticed how you've sort of taken to the place and helped out with the chores. No one expected you to, other than earning your keep in the field, and you've done more than that."

Rob glanced at her bare feet poking from under her sundress as he reached for several bolls near the bottom of the bush. They were caked with dirt, and she had a scratch across her left ankle.

"You mind my being here?"

"No, whatever gave you that idee?" She bobbed up to laugh at him across the bush. Rob moved to the next bush and she followed.

"Pa's really taken to you, and so have Pete and Lloyd. Especially Lloyd. He likes having someone help with the chores."

"What about your mom," Rob asked, and reached to clean the top of the bush.

"She likes having you here also, except she's worried you might be liking me a little too much."

Rob turned to stare at the face on the opposite side of

the bush. Her freshly washed sundress was again dirt-stained and soaked with perspiration, and her unruly hair seemed to poke from under her bonnet in every direction. She had a smudge across her freckled nose, and a scratch across one cheek. She was perfect.

"Well, do you?"

"Do I what?"

"Like me too much?" Her head disappeared as she picked lower on the bush.

"Yeah, I like you," Rob said and reached for the bottom of the bush. He froze as her face appeared between the plants with a rustling of branches.

"That ain't what I meant, and you know it. Chicken! How much do you like me?"

"Well, I don't know. How do you like someone *too much*? What do you want me to say?"

"You don't know? You mean you don't like me, then?" She looked crestfallen.

"No, I don't mean that at all." Rob stopped picking to study her, as her blue eyes filled with water.

"What I meant was, I've never had a girl ask me before. I don't know how to answer except, yeah…I do like you a lot, Clara Jean."

"More'n the other girls?"

"What other girls?" He turned away to escape her stare.

"The other girls you've made love to."

"What…?" Rob dropped the cotton boll in his hand and looked at her. "I ain't never made love to any girls, Clara Jean. What gave you that idea?"

"Your brother Billy."

"Billy?" Rob scooped the fallen cotton boll into his sack and reached for another on the bush. "Figures. What'd Billy say about me?"

"Nothing about you." Clara continued picking and

kept pace on the opposite side of the bush. "Just that he's been bragging a lot to Lloyd about the women he's been with, that's all."

"So you think, because my brother's that way, I'm gonna be like that too? You can't believe everything Billy says, Clara Jean."

"Then, he ain't been with all them women like he says, and is just telling Lloyd a bunch of whoppers. Is that it?" She pulled back a branch to grin, then let it go, almost hitting Rob in the face.

"I didn't say he hasn't been with a bunch of women. It's just that I don't know what he's been telling Lloyd. I've only been traveling with Billy for this past month. I reckon he's been with some women. We got run out of Douglass because he was sleeping with the storekeeper's wife. Henry got mad and came after Billy with a shotgun, and Billy shot him, right there in the middle of the street." Rob paused his picking as she poked her head between the bushes.

"That did happen, then. Did he kill him?"

"No, but we got run out of town just the same."

"If Billy was sleeping with his wife and did the shooting, why'd you get run off? You didn't have anything to do with it, did you?"

"No, but I'm Billy's brother. Besides," Rob stood to pick higher on the bush, "we sold our farm, and I didn't have any place to go, except with Billy."

They stripped the bolls from the next two bushes in silence before Clara pushed the branches aside to stand close and look him in the face.

"Ma says she's seen you watching me."

"Huh?"

"You heard me, Rob Mayfield. Ma says she's seen you watching me while I do my chores. Is that true?"

Rob returned to picking in silence as the girl stood close enough to touch.

"I ain't gonna pick another piece of cotton until you answer me, Rob Mayfield. Have you been watching me?"

"Yeah, I reckon it's true."

"Why?"

He turned to face her as the inside of his stomach did funny things.

"Well, I don't know. I guess I like watching you, Clara Jean. Do you mind?"

"No, I don't mind if you watch me do my chores," she said with a grin. "Why do you like watching me?"

"I don't know." Sweat dripped from Rob's nose, and he wiped his face on his sleeve. "I just like watching you. That's all."

"Okay." She turned away grinning and they picked in silence. They were nearing the end of the row, when Clara pulled the branches back.

"You can stay here."

"Huh?"

"I said, you can stay here. I know your brother keeps saying as soon as we're through picking cotton and he's feeling better, y'all are moving on. But, you can stay here and work the farm. Pa's been needing help, and he likes you a lot."

She let the branches go with a snap and returned quickly to the cotton. Rob watched her slender back for a long minute as she moved to the next bush, grabbing the white bolls with her leaf-stained fingers.

Yeah, I could stay here with you, Clara Jean. I'd like that a lot.

Chapter 15

"She's real pretty, isn't she little brother?"

Rob's head snapped around to glare at his brother. He was seated on the porch watching Clara Jean feed the chickens when Billy slipped up behind him.

"You leave her alone, Billy! You've caused enough trouble, so leave her alone."

"Easy, little brother, easy," he said waving his hands in surrender. He took a seat next to Rob and watched the girl for a long minute. "I meant she's real pretty for you, not me. She's not my type."

"I didn't know you had a type."

"I don't normally, but I've been watching you moon over her, so I'll leave that maverick for you to brand. Besides, this one's too sweet, and she's got cotton in her veins like you." He laughed as Rob glared in anger.

"I meant it as a compliment. She's pretty in a farmer sort of way, and you know how I hate farming of any kind, so she's off limits to me."

"You're sick."

"Oh, Lord, that hurts." Billy held his ribs, laughing.

Chapter 16

Billy Mayfield woke shortly after daybreak, washed, shined his boots, and dressed. He wore his best white shirt with ruffles running the length of the buttons and around each sleeve. He brushed the lint from his black vest, then, went into the kitchen for coffee.

"My, my. Aren't we all duded up for something," Hildegard Russell said with a short laugh. The woman was washing breakfast dishes and didn't break her stride as she continued talking. "Doesn't look like we can count on you helping in the fields today."

"No, I thought I'd ride into town and see if I could stir something up. Where is everybody?"

"In the field. Where'd you expect them to be? If you want to see working folks around here in the mornings, you have to get yourself up early." She finished the last plate and grabbed a towel.

"The coffee's on the stove, and I saved you some bacon and biscuits. They're on a plate inside the oven. You know where the mugs are, so help yourself. I've got to get out there myself."

"I thought you were almost finished. What's the big rush?" Billy glanced at the woman over his shoulder as he poured the coffee.

"We are mostly finished, except for six acres running along the creek. Ted rode over to Harvard Switch before daybreak to see about getting our cotton ginned. They said a train had just come through, and the conductor claimed it was raining up north, which means we've got to get it picked and into the gin before it hits us. That creek floods, and there won't be no cotton left to pick. We could use your help driving the wagons. We stand to lose a lot, if those wagons get rained on."

Billy paused with a biscuit stuffed with several pieces of bacon halfway to his mouth and laughed.

"Me, go back to Harvard Switch? You've got to be joking!"

"Oh, I almost forgot." Hildegard finished drying her hands and hung the towel on a peg next to the sink. "That man's still looking to pinch your head off for messin' with his daughter, isn't he?"

"You might put it that way," Billy said, and toasted her with his mug of coffee.

"Well, how about you helping me and Clara pick, while your brother takes the wagons to the gin?"

"Me pick cotton," Billy said with a laugh. "That'll be the day."

"And what makes you too good to pick?" Hildegard stood at the edge of the table and glared.

"When I left that patch of dirt my folks called a farm, I promised myself I'd never pick another boll of cotton. And that is one promise I plan to keep."

"I see," she said, untying her apron. She grabbed her poke bonnet and tied it under her chin. "Well, if you can't drive the wagons, and you refuse to pick cotton, what do you plan on doing while the rest of us work, Mr. Mayfield?"

"Like I said, I thought I ride into Pittsburg and see what I can stir up." "Hmm, going into town dressed like that, you'll be stirring up something no-good, is more like it. What's the idee of wearing those fancy clothes, anyway? You trying to get folks to notice you?"

"Yes, Ma'am," Billy said with a grin. "It seems to work for King Fisher. Why not me? You've heard of him, I suppose?"

She paused at the door to stare him up and down. "Yes, I know Johnny. I reckon you want to be just like him?"

"Wait," he said as she opened the door. "You *know* John King Fisher?"

"Yes, Ted and I knew his parents, Jobe and Lucinda. Why?"

"I've never actually met him. What's he like?"

Hildegard stared at the excited youth a long minute before replying.

"Johnny's a good-looking young man, pretty much like you. He started out okay, but somehow got swollen up with himself, thinking he can get away with most anything. Up to now, he mostly has. Stealing horses and cattle and killing folks. Just like you, he wears fancy clothes to catch folk's attention. That answer your question?"

"When was the last time you saw him?"

"You might be able to lay around all day, but I've got work to do."

"I know, I know," Billy said, "but I'd like to meet him someday."

"Yes, you probably would." Hildegard's stare grew cold as she continued.

"Johnny turned out to be a no-good roughneck just like his friend, Ben Thompson. Now, that he's gotten married and has four daughters, and somehow gotten himself elected sheriff of Uvalde County, I suppose he's still a no good roughneck. We saw John King Fisher last March down in Austin, when we went to a funeral for Ted's sister. He was all duded up with a Mexican sombrero that had a gold band. He had on an embroidered vest and silk shirt with crimson sashes. He was even wearing chaps made out of tiger skin. He had fancy guns sort of like yours, only he had silver-mounted holsters, and silver spurs with little bells that jingled when he walked. Oh, everyone knew when John

King Fisher walked into the room alright. He was down-right pretty. Pretty as a rattlesnake. That's what you want to be like, boy?"

"Well now," Billy said with a grin, "that doesn't sound too bad, does it? He's rich and owns a big ranch. You also said he got married and has children, and is even a lawman. And, oh," he added as she pulled the door open, "I'll need my guns before I go to town."

"What for? There isn't any need for wearing them, unless you plan on killing someone."

"Well, I don't plan on doing that, but you never know what might happen."

Hildegard pulled a skeleton key from a tobacco tin and opened the hall closet. "Here," she said, handing him the gunbelt and matching set of pistols. "Don't get yourself killed."

"Why, thank you Ma'am. I didn't really think you cared," Billy said with a snicker.

"When it comes to you, I don't. I was thinking about your brother. He's a nice boy, and I don't want to see him hurt."

"I don't want that either," he said, strapping on the gunbelt. "That's why I decided to look after him when our ma died. He's the only family I've got."

"Look after him? The best thing you could do for that boy is leave him here while you go chasing all over creation."

"Well, now. You'd like that, wouldn't you?" He grabbed his hat and dusted the brim. "You'd have a big strong boy to pick cotton and work like a slave for next to nothing."

"Is that what you think? Is that why you think Ted and I would like it if Rob decided to stay with us," Hildegard yelled.

"Yes, Ma'am. That's exactly what I think," Billy said

with a smirk. "I promised myself I'd never pick cotton again. And when I came back to get Rob, I promised to do the same for him. I kind of broke that promise when that big nigger beat the hell out of me. But I aim to see it never happens again." He adjusted his hat with a grin and headed toward the barn.

"You're gonna get the both of you killed! You hear me?"

"Yes, Ma'am," Billy said loudly with a tip of his hat. "But at least everyone will know who we are, by the time I'm finished."

Chapter 17

Rob felt a drop of rain as the heavy wagon creaked and groaned its way toward the huge pole barn adjacent to Hard Ivory's steam cotton gin. There were approximately a dozen wagons already parked under the protection of the barn, and Rob halted his team of mules in the open, while a young boy guided Theodore Russell inside. A second boy ran to untie Rob's horse from the rear of the wagon, and tie it to a hitching rail next to Theodore's. He felt several more drops against his cheek before they had unhitched Theodore's team, and the first lad yelled and waved at Rob.

"Here! Bring it right over next to yer pa's. Come on, now."

Rob parked his wagon tightly next to Theodore's, and began unhitching the team as the boy lent a hand. Rob guessed him to be around twelve, but stout for his size. His dark skin glistened with perspiration as they led the team toward Theodore.

"You and your pa had best get the rest of your wagons over and inside the barn, 'cause it shore enough is coming. And them that gets their wagons here first, are gonna be the ones that gets to park inside. The rest is jus' gonna have to leave 'em in the rain."

"Thanks." Rob gave him a friendly pat on the back.

"Don't mention it," he said, and quickly turned to yell at another waiting wagon. "Come on, don't jus' sit there."

"We'd best listen to what he says," Theodore said, climbing onto his horse.

"Yes sir. I've already felt a few drops." Rob handed Theodore the lead rope to his mule team, and mounted his own horse.

"Me too. We'd better rustle, or these other yahoos are gonna take all the room in Ivory's pole barn. I just hope Hildie's got the lower eight picked." Theodore kicked his horse in the flanks with a yell and started down the road at a fast trot. Rob felt several more drops as he urged his horse and team to follow.

The drops of rain were coming more frequent and regular by the time they reached the farm. Rob jumped off his horse and helped Clara empty her cotton sack in the wagon before hitching the team of mules. They had the lower eight picked, except for two rows planted near the creek bank.

"Better forget them last two rows and dump your sacks," Theodore yelled.

"It won't take us long to pick two rows, Pa," Lloyd protested in a loud voice.

"Maybe, but it's a coming, son. Better to lose a couple of rows, than a whole wagon. Dump your sack and help me tarp it down. Then, y'all better get to the house and care for the animals. This might be a good one by the look of the sky."

The wagon was two-thirds filled when they had emptied the remaining sacks. Rob helped pull and tie off the canvas tarp, then climbed into the seat and grabbed the reins before staring down at Theodore.

"I can handle the last wagon, Mr. Russell. Go take care of things at the house with Mrs. Russell."

"You sure, boy?"

"Yes, Sir. I'm sure."

"I reckon I will." Rob released the brake and paused as

Clara climbed into the wagon next to him. Several

large drops splashed against the brim of his hat as he stared at the girl.

"Better get moving like Pa's says, or you'll get stuck right here in the field," she said as he continued staring.

"You'd best be heading toward the house with your ma. No sense in you getting wet too."

"Would you like me to drive? I can handle a team as good as Pa."

"You're not going to the house, are you," he said as she reached for the reins.

"Nope."

"Well, here, give me those," he took the reins and gave them a shake, "better hang on. Ya! Get up there, you lazy jackasses!"

"Pa says one of us had better go along in case Mr. Ivory sees you. His daughter is missing."

"Wilma Ivory's missing?"

"Yeah, she ran off, and her pa thinks she's joined up with your brother. They're afraid if Mr. Ivory sees you, he might decide on pounding you senseless in place of your brother," Clara said with grin.

"Hmm, never thought of that. Ya! Get up there," he yelled as the team pulled up the embankment and onto the road. "Why didn't he come, if he was afraid of Mr. Ivory stomping a mud hole through me?"

"He wants to see things are taken care of, before the storm hits. Besides, Mr. Ivory took a liking to me last season. He said I was polite and had good manners, for a white child. Pa figures I'd probably stop him from pounding you with a smile, quicker than he could." She glanced at him sideways and laughed.

"Your pa's right."

The banter continued as the wagon creaked and bumped its way toward Harvard. The scattered raindrops had turned into a steady sprinkle of large, cold drops by the time they turned off the road toward Ivory's cotton gin. The boy ran out of the barn yelling and waving.

"Pull it right here! Come on, next to Carson Burnett's wagon."

Rob brought the wagon to a halt in the vacant spot the boy had directed him to, and began unhitching the team as the young man continued talking.

"Y'all got here jus' in time. Ain't but a couple places left, and the rain's shore a coming."

"That's what my pa says," Clara said, while digging around under the wagon seat.

"Your pa's right. You're gonna get yourself wet heading home," the boy said with a firm nod. "You got yourself a slicker?"

"Yes, sir, right here." She pulled two oilcloth rain slickers from under the seat and tossed one of them to Rob. "Here, don't want you catching cold. One sick Mayfield is enough to take care of."

"Ain't nothing wrong with my brother, 'cept he's sick in the head," Rob said, pulling the slicker over his head.

"You said it, I didn't." Clara pulled her slicker on and turned toward the boy holding their team in check.

"Thanks," she squeezed his hand in a firm shake. "Tell Mr. Ivory my pa will be in to settle up with him in a day or two."

"Yes, Ma'am, I shore will." He led the team to the edge of the barn to stare at the steady drops falling from the sky. "You're shore gonna get wet."

"Yes, I think you're right," Rob said, helping Clara onto her father's horse. The boy holding the team turned his head as she took her time adjusting her long skirt, which kept riding up to reveal her stockinged ankles.

"Better hurry, farm boy. Your friend is right, it's starting to rain pretty hard, now." She grinned at Rob and nudged the horse forward with her heels.

Rob mounted his own horse and, taking the lead rope from the boy with a "much obliged," followed. The mules balked at the rain, so he had to tie the lead rope to his saddle horn and give his horse and extra kick to get them to follow. He caught up with Clara, but not much was said on the return trip, other than a few remarks about how the rain would cause the creek to rise, washing out the remaining cotton. She placed a hand against Rob's arm and brought her horse to a halt as the house and barn came into sight.

"What's wrong," Rob asked, giving the farm a quick survey to spot any trouble.

"Nothing. It's just something I've been wanting to do." She slipped her hand up to the back of his neck and pulled him close to kiss him on the mouth. Rob thought his heart might leap from his chest as their lips clung together. Then, just as quickly, she released her hold and nudged her horse forward.

He sat watching the girl and horse through the vale of raindrops. It was his first kiss, other than what he had received from his mother, but it was sure different somehow. He nudged his horse forward as his heart continued pounding. His entire body tingled and he wanted nothing more than to take Clara Jean in his arms and squeeze her body next to his, and kiss every inch of her freckled face, but especially her lips.

Chapter 18

The longed-for rain never came, although lightening danced across the sky, and thunder rolled with a vengeance. It was as if the gods of nature were trying to forewarn that the year-long drought would continue. Rob watched from the back porch as a sheet of lightening crackled across the afternoon sky, followed by a clap of thunder that caused the dog to crowd close to Rob's feet with a whimper.

"Worried about your brother?"

"Pardon?" Theodore's voice had given Rob a start.

"I asked if you're worried about that brother of yours?" The big man handed Rob a steaming mug of coffee, then took a sip from his own.

"No," he shook his head, "I wasn't even thinking about him." There was no way of telling the man he had been reliving the kiss his daughter had given him for the hundredth time.

"Well, don't. He's probably holed up next to a warm fire someplace."

"Holed up next to a card table inside some saloon, if I know my brother."

"Hmm," Theodore snorted and took another sip. "Guess you know your brother then."

"I don't expect we'll be seeing him anytime soon. He doesn't like getting dirty, especially those fancy boots of his. He's always shining them, even when we were on the trail. I asked him about it once, and he said that keeping a good image was everything."

"Well now," Theodore said with a snigger, "I reckon looking pretty might be important to some folks, but people can usually see through that in a hurry. It's what's inside a man that makes the real difference. Folks will cotton to them they can count on when the chips are down...not them that just look pretty.

"Take you for instance." He continued as he set his coffee mug on a wooden box and began packing his pipe. "I never asked you to take that last wagon to Harvard, but you did, knowing full-well Hard Ivory might beat the stuffings out of you because of what your brother did. You did it 'cause it needed doing. That's something that's inside of you, and it'll make you a better man than your brother ever dreamed of being."

"Oh, Billy's ornery alright. There's times I'd like to take a ridgepole to his head. But he ain't all bad," Rob said.

"I don't reckon anyone's *all* bad son," Theodore said with a chuckle. "Most people's got some sort of redeeming quality, it's just that we ain't seen your brother's redeeming side. Why don't you tell me something good about Billy?"

"Well, he came back to take care of me after our ma died."

"Really." Theodore paused as he lit his pipe. "Go on. What else is good about him?"

"He says he's gonna take me to New Orleans, and show me some of the fancy places he's been to."

"Hmm, last time I checked, New Orleans is back that away." Theodore pointed over his shoulder with his pipe stem. "I think you're headed the wrong way."

"Well, Billy said we couldn't go down there broke, so we had to make some money before we went." Rob took a sip of coffee as he eyed the man puffing intently on the pipe.

"Well," Theodore said, releasing a cloud of tobacco smoke, "that's a new idee coming from him. I offered him a job right here on this farm, same as you, and he turned me down. How's he planning on making this money?"

Rob stared at the trees dancing in the wind before answering.

"No, Billy doesn't like cotton, or farming in general. He left our farm several years ago, swearing he'd never plow or pick again. I don't know what he's got in mind. He likes to gamble. Maybe he plans on doing it with cards."

"Mmmm." Theodore beat the ashes from his pipe against the steps and watched the wind blow them away. "Cards are a risky business at best. Never knew an honest card player to make a dime. You'd better stick to farming, son. You might not get rich, but it's a lot safer, and you'll close your eyes at night with a clear conscience."

"Yes, sir," Rob said over his shoulder as Theodore went back inside with their empty mugs.

******

It was nine o'clock, after the dinner dishes had been washed and tucked inside the cupboard, when she joined him. Clara Jean Russell had washed the day's dirt away and donned a freshly ironed flower sack dress with a small blue flower print. Her blond hair was pulled back and tied with a blue ribbon, and she smelled of lilac perfume.

"Hello, farm boy, what are you up to?" Her bare arm gently brushed against him as she looked into the blackness of the night.

"Nothing much. Just watching the lightning."

"Worried about your brother?"

"Billy? Na," Rob shook his head, "he won't be out in that storm getting his boots dirty. I'm just thinking."

"About what?" She slipped a hand under his arm and leaned against his shoulder.

"Us...this afternoon."

"What about this afternoon?"

"You know." Her presence and smell caused his heart

66

to pound.

"No, I don't know." She tilted her head to look up at him. "Tell me, Rob Mayfield. What do you remember about this afternoon?"

"I...I...it's just that..." He was sure she could hear his pounding chest as beads of sweat appeared on his brow.

"Hmmm," she set her lips in a thin line and nodded, "my cat stole your tongue, is that it, Rob Mayfield? What's a girl got to do in order for you to tell her how you feel about her?"

"Clara Jean, I...you don't know..." he stammered at her grinning face.

"No I don't. Why don't you tell me?"

"I...I..."

"Cat still got your tongue?" She glanced past Rob's shoulder toward the empty living room. "Well, why don't you show me then?"

Her lips drew close enough for Rob to feel her breath as her slender body moved against his. His hands seemed to take a mind of their own as they slid to her waist, feeling her ribs through the soft cotton dress, then sliding to her back and pressing her against his chest. Her lips found his in a long, tender kiss that caused him to tingle. She broke the kiss by laying her head against his chest and hugging him with strong arms.

"Now, what do you think about this afternoon, Rob Mayfield?"

"I think I'm in love with you, Clara Jean." His voice was no more than a whisper, and he wasn't sure she had heard him over the wind whipping the trees, until she heaved a sigh and took his cheeks in her hands.

"Now, that wasn't too hard was it? I love you, too." She gave him a quick kiss and ran inside the house.

He stood frozen for what seemed an eternity, before gulping a deep breath. "Oh, Lord!" He opened the screen door and stood in the wind with his face tilted to the heavens. He refrained from shouting, for fear of waking the entire family, but Rob Mayfield felt as though he had been reborn. The most beautiful woman in the world, Clara Jean Russell, loved him.

Chapter 19

"I ain't arguing about that, woman," Theodore growled at his wife. "I know he's a nice boy, and a hard worker to boot. He loves the land, and that means a lot. I'm just being cautious 'bout this thing with Clara Jean. I don't think it's right."

"You wouldn't think it was right if she fell in love with a saint, because she's your daughter," Hildegard said with a cackle. She scooped the eggs she'd been frying onto a plate and slid it in front of her husband. "Here, eat your eggs and leave them alone."

"I still say it ain't right. I don't like that brother of his, and that's all there is to it." He finished by stuffing half an egg into his mouth and chewing vigorously.

"She isn't in love with Billy Mayfield. She's in love with Rob, who happens to be a nice boy." Hildegard sipped her coffee and stared at her husband intently.

"I don't happen to like his brother either, but that's not the point. In fact, I've never liked Tom, but that didn't keep me from marrying you."

"Ya don't?"

"Nope, never did," Hildegard said, shaking her head.

"What's the matter with Tom?"

"I think he's irritating. The point I'm trying to make is, my not liking your brother didn't keep me from loving you, or ruin our chances for a happy marriage. I'm glad she had the courage to slip into our room last night and tell us she's fallen in love with this boy."

"Hmmm." Theodore shoved the last of the eggs into his mouth and washed them down with coffee. "I'm still agin' it. She's too young. He's too young for that matter."

"Ted Russell, you old hypocrite!" Hildegard laughed. "I was exactly the same age when you asked me to marry you."

"And we didn't get married for another year, when you turned sixteen."

"Yes, and they're not asking to get married, are they? All she said was, they are in love, plain and simple. We can ask them to wait, if it ever gets to that point."

"It was different with us, Hildie, and you know it. We were more grown up back then. These two are different. They're still children." His face grew red as his wife roared with laughter.

"Oh, Lord Almighty! Have you actually *looked* at your daughter lately? Her body is filling out, Ted. Maybe they are young, but as far as being *grown up*, they both worked like slaves getting our cotton picked and to the gin. If you want to know the truth, Clara Jean has always worked like a slave from the time she could barely walk, and never complained. I think we owe her the respect she deserves. In fact, we owe them both, Ted." She reached across the table and gripped his hand.

"Whether you know it or not, its Clara's mating season. Her body's changing, and she's feeling things she's never felt before. It might be hard for you to understand, but women are like that. Rob Mayfield is the first available young man to come along. He's the *only* boy around, except for her two brothers. She's going to have strong feelings about him. Don't break her heart by telling her she's too young, and she can't fall in love with him. Please?"

"I reckon I understand more'n you think, Hildie. Boys feel the same sort of things when they start turning into men. And I'm not worried about my breaking her heart, it's *him* breaking her heart I'm worrying about. What if he doesn't stick around? What if he takes off with that brother of his, and goes to New Orleans?"

"I guess that's the chance we'll have to take, isn't it? Everyone has to take that chance when their children start growing up and falling in love. It's funny, isn't it?"

"What is?" Theodore rose from the table to refill their coffee mugs.

"We take the chance of breaking our own hearts when we're young and falling in love. Then, we repeat that chance when our children enter that phase of their lives. I never realized what my mother must have gone through watching me grow, until this minute."

"Okay, Hildie, for you," Theodore toasted his wife with his coffee. "I'll sit back and let nature take its course for you and Clara Jean. But I'm not promising I won't take a buggy whip to that boy's backside if he breaks my little girl's heart."

"I'll help you if that happens." She smiled and returned the toast.

Chapter 20

Rob could smell the aroma long before reaching the screen door. The heavy wind had stopped sometime during the night, and he awoke at daybreak to gray skies and a gentle breeze. The temperature had fallen, bringing a sharp nip to the air. After downing a mug of steaming coffee and gobbling a plate of eggs, bacon and two hot buttered biscuits, he waded through a herd of clucking chickens to care for the animals inside the barn. It was on his return trip the smell of hot peach pie accosted his nostrils. After scraping his boots against a metal rail attached to the steps, he stomped his feet and allowed the screen door to slam shut behind him.

"Smells good. What is it," he asked as Clara poked her head through the door and smiled. She had a smudge of flour on her left cheek and across her nose. *Yeah*, he thought, *I saw you looking just like that, smudge and all, before arriving here several weeks ago.* Clara Jean was the same girl he'd dreamed about after long hot days of plowing and hoeing cotton on their farm outside Douglass. Those dreams were so real, he could feel her in his arms and taste her kisses. He had never actually seen the person of Clara Jean Russell, but he had known her long before arriving at the Russell farm.

"Thanks. I'm baking a peach pie. My own special recipe."

"Peaches? Where'd you get peaches this time of year?" Rob removed his manure-caked boots and began washing his face and hands.

"Me and Ma can a bunch every summer. We've got a cellar full of canned peaches, apples, cured hams...most anything a person needs. Pa says there's no need of going hungry during the winter, when you can grow things in the summer."

"Your pa's right," Rob said, drying his hands and face. He paused to grin. "It's a good thing you've got all those things stored, 'cause the smell of your cooking sure makes a fellow hungry."

"She doesn't do that very often," Hildegard yelled from inside. "She must think you're somehow special, Rob Mayfield." The woman appeared behind her daughter in the doorway. "Clara Jean only cooks her peach pie on special occasions, such as church socials, or when we're going to have important company. Are you important, Rob Mayfield?"

The question took Rob by surprise, and he stuttered and stumbled, looking for an answer.

"I...I...don't know. I...I...ask Clara J...Jean... I..."

"Of course he's important," Clara laughed and swatted at her mother. "Quit being so mean, Ma!"

Her mother laughed and disappeared, only to reappear. "Clara's secret recipe is a shot of her father's brandy mixed in with the peaches." The woman vanished a second time, leaving them alone on the porch.

"Brandy?"

"Uh-huh," she said with a nod. "Pastor McElroy loves my pie."

"If it tastes half as good as it smells, it's going to be delicious."

"It is." She came out onto the porch and closed the door. "I told my parents about us last night."

Rob felt a chill sweep across his spine.

"You told your father I kissed you?"

"Maybe, I don't know if I got that far," she said with

a giggle. "I told them you said you love me, and that I love you, too."

"What'd they say?" Rob glanced around, praying her father wasn't standing somewhere with a shotgun in his hands.

"Ma acted like she expected it to happen, and Pa growled about me being too young. Ma told him to hush his mouth and that she thinks you're a nice boy. He agreed that you're nice enough, but he still thinks we're too young for such things. I heard them fussing about it again this morning in the kitchen, but I think it's going to be okay. Pa likes you a lot, Rob. So does Ma and both my brothers. I hope you like them too."

"Like them? I think they're great. They are what I wished my family was like, if I had any. Billy's the only family I've got, and I ain't seen him in two days. I don't even know where he is."

"Do you care?" She moved closer.

"Yeah, some. He's my brother."

"Billy will be leaving soon. You know that, don't you?" She waited for his nod. "Are you going with him, Rob?"

"I want to stay here with you, Clara Jean. I told you last night that I love you, and I meant every word of it."

Her entire face seemed to explode into a smile as she leaped on him, throwing her arms around his neck and crushing his lips with a kiss. Rob's heart raced as he slipped his arm around her slender body and returned the kiss.

"Hey, cut that out!"

The voice caused Rob to release his hold and stagger backward in his stocking feet.

"Oh hush, Lloyd," Clara snapped at her grinning brother. "You liked to scared the dickens outta us!"

"Better not let Pa catch you kissing him like that, or he'll take a hickory switch to your backside. No telling what he'll do to Rob." The boy laughed as he scraped manure from his boots.

"Pa's not going to do nothing to me or Rob, 'cause I've already told him we're in love."

"Think so? Try doing that in front of him, and see what happens." Lloyd let the screen door slam shut and removed his boots. "Bet you an extra piece of your pie you won't kiss him in front of Mom and Dad."

"That ain't much of a bet. You'll get a piece of pie regardless of whether I have the courage to kiss Rob in front of Dad or not. What do I get if I do?"

"A kiss from your boyfriend." He grinned at them both and entered the house laughing.

"Jesus Lord Almighty," Rob said, exhaling a gush of air. "He liked to scared me to death sneaking up on us like that."

"He didn't *sneak*. We just weren't paying any attention." Clara glanced around quickly before kissing Rob one more time.

"There," she said patting his chest. "That finishes what I started. Now, I've got to check on the pie."

She disappeared inside the house, leaving Rob Mayfield stunned, and standing on the screened porch in his sock feet.

Chapter 21

Billy Mayfield took his time rolling and lighting his cigarette, then leaned back to study the cards in his hand. He had arrived in Pittsburg two days ago with not more than ten dollars in his pocket. That was before wind turned the street in front of Stella's Saloon into a dust storm. Not wanting to spend all he had on a room and a couple of meals, Bill left his horse and saddle at the livery and headed straight toward Stella's in hope of finding a friendly poker game. Since that time, his ten dollars had turned into more than two hundred, and he was certain the small straight he was holding would increase it by another thirty.

He placed his hand face-down on the table and studied the men seated around the table. The young man on his left was not much older than Billy, and had more than likely played cards with his friends at home or behind the schoolhouse. He was awkward and stood to lose the last of his money on this very hand. The man seated next to the boy was a large farmer dressed in faded coveralls who sweated profusely. He played better than the young boy, but was in way over his head, having played most of the day and well into the night, while borrowing money from several friends. Those friends were gone now, and the last of his money was on the table. The one seated on Billy's right had taken the place of another player that had gone bust not more than half an hour ago, and was only in the game for fun. Billy knew the type, and knew the man would leave before losing any serious money.

"Cards anyone?" Billy thumbed the deck as he studied their faces.

"Four," the young boy said.

"Four it is." Billy peeled four cards as the boy tossed his discards to the center of the table. Several spectators chuckled. "Must've not given you anything on the deal. Sorry 'bout that."

"I'll take two," the coverall-clad man growled, "and make 'em good ones."

"Yes, sir. Two for our friend across the table." Billy peeled off two cards and tossed them toward the man, who instantly jumped to his feet and pointed a gun across the table.

"I said good ones, and from the top of the deck!" Several tables cleared among a clatter of scraping chairs and curses, leaving Billy and the angry farmer alone.

"Aw come on Harry, put that away. It's only a game." The voice came from someone near the bar.

"Shut up! This is between me and this card cheat." He waved the gun in small circles and yelled. "I said, I want two good cards from the top of the deck, now!"

Billy calmly took a drag from his cigarette before crushing it under the toe of his boot, then rose from the table with his hands in the air.

"I reckon you must be upset about losing yours and your friend's money. Is that it?"

"You bet it is, and you've been cheating all along. Now, I want two cards from the top of that deck, and a chance to win all my money back."

"Well, I've been called a lot of things, but never a card cheat," Billy said glancing around the saloon. His manner caused several people to chuckle. "What makes you think I'm a cheat?"

"Nobody plays as good as you do without cheating."

"Oh, I beg to differ with you, friend." Billy picked up

his drink with his right hand and turned his left side slightly away from the angry farmer. His manner was so smooth the farmer didn't notice when Billy loosed the thong holding his left pistol in the holster. "I lived in New Orleans for awhile, and I met and knew quite a few gamblers who were better than me. In fact, I asked one of them to teach me. That's why I'm better than you are." He toasted the man and took a sip.

"Now, are you going to apologize for calling me a cheat so we can finish our game? Or, are you going to force me to kill you in front of God and all these people?"

The man paled as he glanced around the room, looking for some support.

"They have nothing to do with this, friend. It's between you and me. You called me a card cheat. Are you going to take it back and finish our game, or make me kill you?"

"My hell, Harry! Tell the man you're sorry and put the gun away," the bartender yelled. Billy calmly slid his left pistol from its holster as the man glanced around him one last time.

"No," he shouted and cocked the hammer on his gun.

Billy was still holding the drink in his right hand when he pulled the trigger. The blast from his pistol sent the farmer pitching backward, where he landed on the next table and rolled to the floor. His gun discharged harmlessly toward the ceiling as he fell.

A man with two-days' growth of stubble ran to kneel beside the body. He laid a hand across the farmer's chest and listened for a few seconds before staring at Billy with wide eyes. "Jesus Christ! You killed him!" The saloon was instantly engulfed in chatter.

"Hell yes, I killed him," Bill said and downed his drink in one gulp. "He would've killed me if I didn't."

"Okay, game's over boys, collect your money." The woman who spoke was attractive and middle-aged, with strawberry blond hair. Billy might have been interested in Stella West, but for the fact she was twice his age and had a manner as hard as the Texas ground his father had plowed. "I'm closing the place until Sheriff Coffee has a look." She turned a set of cold blue eyes on Billy.

"You're staying until Coffee says you're free, then you take your game somewhere else. You're not welcome here."

"Why? Would I have been welcome if I'd let him kill me?" Billy snorted.

"No, but your kind always attracts trouble. You come in here with your ruffled shirts, fancy vest and shiny boots, then start dealing cards like a riverboat gambler. Yeah," she nodded, "I know your kind, and you're always trouble. I've got no way of proving it, but I wouldn't be surprised if you were cheating. I run a friendly place for folks who live around here. Harry may have been a bad loser, but people liked him and he was a good customer. When Sheriff Coffee gets finished, you collect your winnings and git."

"Yes Ma'am, I had planned on doing just that," he said with a laugh.

Billy Mayfield calmly reloaded the empty chamber in his pistol and collected his winnings, then ordered another drink from the bar as he waited for the sheriff. The witnesses waiting to tell their story cast glances his way and talked in hushed tones. *Yeah*, he thought as he sipped the drink. He was on his way. People in Douglass, Harvard, and now Pittsburg knew who Bill Mayfield was. It wouldn't be long before Rob would start earning a name also. Rob had been a little reluctant to change up to now, but he'd get him some new clothes and a gun with the money he'd just won. Then, with a little instruction, and Rob would be okay. Pretty soon, all of Texas would both know and remember the Mayfield boys for something besides cotton. Billy Mayfield was more than surprised when Sheriff Oscar J. Coffee locked him in a cell.

Chapter 22

Rob was busy feeding the mules when the man rode into the yard and stopped. Theodore and Hildegard were stacking firewood on the porch. He was too far away to hear the conversation, but from the way Clara's parents were acting, the news couldn't have been good. He decided it would be best if he stayed at the corral with the mules instead of poking his nose into an upsetting situation. He was surprised when Theodore stormed off the porch and marched in a beeline toward the corral.

"Best come to the house and gather your brother's things," Theodore growled as he took the pitchfork Rob was using and gave it a toss.

"Why, what's wrong?" Rob rushed to match the man's stride back to the house.

"Your brother shot and killed a man inside Stella's Saloon. The sheriff's got him locked up in jail." He paused as they reached the steps and placed a hand on Rob's shoulder. "Might as well pack your things too."

"Huh?" Rob was stunned. He could hear Clara's wail from inside the kitchen.

"No, Mama! He can't leave. Please!"

"The man Bill shot has a passel of brothers, and Sheriff Coffee doesn't want anymore killing. He's ordering both you boys to leave Pittsburg now…today. So get your things."

Rob looked toward the man who had arrived less than five minutes earlier. He'd never seen him before, but he would never forget him. He was large and heavyset, with a potbelly and graying hair. He held his hat in his hands and shook his sad head slowly.

"Sorry, son. I ain't got nothing to do with it. I only brung the news."

"Why do I have to leave? I've never been to town." Rob's voice sounded distant and foreign as he spoke.

"I don't know," the stranger said. "Better ask the sheriff when you get to town."

The screen door burst open with a bang as Clara Jean flew past her father and threw her arms around Rob, almost knocking him to the ground.

"Oh God, don't go. Please don't leave me," she cried, and covered his face with kisses. Rob was only able to return one kiss before her father pried them apart.

"Rob's gotta go to town and get things settled with Sheriff Coffee, honey. He'll come back whenever the sheriff says he can. Won't you, boy?" He finished by giving Rob a serious nod.

"Yeah, sure," Rob said, as her father pulled her toward the house. "He couldn't keep me away."

"I love you. Please don't go," Clara cried as Hildegard folded her in her arms.

"I love you too, Clara Jean. I'll be coming back. I promise."

"Better collect your things and get going," Theodore said, slapping Rob on the shoulder.

******

Clara Jean Russell wiped her nose against her sleeve as she watched Rob Mayfield disappear behind the row of trees lining the creek. He promised he would be returning as soon as Sheriff Coffee said he could, but the empty hole inside her breast couldn't understand such words.

"I'm sure he'll be coming back when this all dies down, honey," Hildegard said as she squeezed her daughter's shoulder. "Don't you think so, Ted?"

"Oh, sure. That boy loves this farm and our little girl as much as we do. In fact, I wouldn't be surprised if…"

"I need to feed the chickens," she said, cutting her father off in mid-sentence as she pulled from her mother's grip.

She knew her parents were only trying to make her feel better, but that was an impossible task. She felt entirely removed from her body as she scooped a pan full of feed from a sack, and scattered it. Lloyd paused with a pitchfork full of hay to give her a knowing look. He was finishing Rob's job. Peter stood at the corner of the house with the dog, staring. She didn't want or need their pity, any more than she needed her parent's words. Clara Jean only wanted Rob Mayfield, but he was gone.

Chapter 23

The five mile ride to Pittsburg seemed to take an eternity. The pain Rob Mayfield felt was similar to what he had experienced when his mother died, but somehow different. He knew his Ma was dead and not coming back, and it was no one's fault. Things like that just happened. But Clara Jean Russell was alive. He could still feel her arms around him and the heaving of her body as she sobbed. He felt her lips against his cheeks and mouth as she kissed him repeatedly, and could taste her tears as he kissed her back. He could even smell her hair. She had baked bread that very morning.

Rob remembered reading about a young boy who fell into a dry well a few years earlier and died. He was haunted for weeks, wondering what it must have been like, trapped inside a dark hole with no way out. He could picture the boy screaming, crying, yelling, and even trying to claw his way out, but nobody heard him. He felt as though he had somehow fallen into such a hole, with happiness and Clara Jean just out of reach, and no way of climbing out.

"Better wipe them tears, boy. We're entering town," the big man said. Rob knew the man had tried introducing himself, but couldn't remember much of what he had said. He thought his name was Darrell something, but wasn't sure.

"Thanks," Rob said, wiping his face against his sleeve.

They trotted their horses down the dusty street past Stella's Saloon and several stores, stopping at the jail.

Billy's horse was saddled and tied at the hitching post in front. Rob noticed several people staring as he slid from the saddle, but the town looked mostly deserted.

"They're at the funeral," Sheriff Coffee said, when Rob mentioned the fact. "That's why I sent Darrell after you, so's I could get you two outta Pittsburg while they are off planting Harry."

"But, why do I have to go? I didn't do nothing," Rob pleaded.

"I know you didn't, boy. And I know Ted and Hildie speak well of you, and that counts for a lot with folks around here. But the fact remains, that brother of your'n shot Harry Lippert deader'n last year's Christmas goose. Now, Harry may have been a lot of things, but one thing he was, was liked. He has three brothers who are looking to even the score. I'm afraid if they can't find your brother, they might come looking for you.

"Now," he continued as he unlocked Billy's cell, "I wouldn't mind it so much if they plugged your smart-mouthed brother. But I'd hate to see you killed for something he did. I'd also hate seeing one of the Russells hurt if they happened to get in the way." He paused and scratched his stubbled chin as he looked Rob over from head to toe.

"I hear little Clara and you sort of have a thing going. How'd you like it if she got herself killed because someone came gunning for you?"

Rob shook his head.

"Didn't think so. I wouldn't like it either. But I'd hate it worse, if I had to lock up or hang someone I've known for years over something this knucklehead started." He pulled the cell door open.

"Come on, fancy pants. I asked the preacher to be long-winded today, but I don't know how long he can hold folks at a funeral." Sheriff Oscar J. Coffee opened a drawer and handed Billy a stack of bills.

"Here's your winnings, minus thirty five dollars."

"Why am I shy thirty five dollars," Bill asked as a crease suddenly appeared between his eyebrows.

"Twenty five dollars for discharging a firearm within the city limits. Another ten dollars for your upkeep inside the jail." The sheriff slammed the drawer closed. "Your guns are hanging on the wall. They're unloaded, and I don't want you loading them until you're outta town. Got that?"

"Yeah, I've got it," Billy said, shoving the money in his pocket. "Ten dollars sounds like a lot for being locked up for one day."

"I run a fancy jail, so quit complaining and get out of town."

"Come on, Billy," Rob said before his brother could argue. "Thank you, Sheriff," he added as Billy brushed past him and out the door.

"You're okay, son. Just get your brother out of town as soon as possible."

"Yes, Sir."

Rob mounted his horse and paused to study the lawman.

"Sir?"

"What is it, son?"

"Do you think I will ever be able to return to the Russell's farm?"

"It's a possibility, when things calm down. I'll tell you what," he said coming to the edge of the sidewalk. "You write me, say in a year or so. I'll tell you when it's safe for you to return. I'll bet that little girl will be waiting."

"Thanks."

"Better get going. I see folks returning from the cemetery."

Rob stole a glance at the buggies and horses entering the far end of town before turning his horse the opposite way and following his brother away from Pittsburg, Texas, and away from Clara Jean Russell. What neither brother saw was the lone horseman under a clump of trees watching them leave. After making sure which direction the brothers had taken, the horseman nudged his brown sorrel back into town and toward the group of mourners returning from the graveyard.

Chapter 24

They had traveled nearly fifteen miles before the full impact of what had taken place hit Rob. He waited until Billy had turned off the trail and dismounted in a heavily wooded area near a small Baptist church. There were a few houses scattered along the road with several children playing with a jump rope in a grassy area near a church. A small hand-painted sign nailed to a tree read, *Hamil's Chapel.*

"Well," Billy said, loosening his saddle cinches, "I don't see any stores, restaurants or saloons. I guess we'll make due with what we've got."

"Why'd you do it, Billy?"

"Do what?"

"Kill that man," Rob yelled. The girls playing jump rope stopped to stare.

"He called me a card cheat and drew a gun on me. What'd you expect me to do? Let him kill me?" Billy gave his saddle a toss onto a bed of leaves.

"It's always the same isn't it, *big brother*," Rob said, giving him a shove on the shoulder.

"Whoa, hold on there, little brother. Guess who you're talking to." Billy returned Rob's shove with one of his own.

"I know full-well who I'm talking to. I'm talking to the same ass that's gotten us thrown out of every town we've been in."

"Every town we've been in?" Billy laughed and turned away to care for his horse.

"Yeah, every town. We got run out of Douglass because you were messing around with Zora and wound up shooting Henry. We got run out of Harvard because you were messing around with Wilma Ivory. Now we get run out of Pittsburg because you killed a man over a card game. When's it gonna end, Billy?" Rob grabbed his brother by the arm and pulled him around. "Huh? Tell me, when's it gonna end?"

"For your information," Billy paused long enough to remove his brother's hand, "Zora Whitefield wanted it just as much as I did, and Henry's a jackass."

"He's her husband!"

"Yeah, and he's also an idiot. Coming after me with a shotgun in the middle of town, putting on a big show, thinking he was gonna scare me or something. He knew we were leaving. All he had to do was keep his mouth shut for ten more minutes, and we would have gone. The town would've forgotten about me and Zora and gone back to their cotton." Billy removed the saddle blanket and hung it across a log to dry.

"I suppose Wilma Ivory wanted it also, huh?"

"Yes, as a matter of fact, she did." Billy squared around to face Rob. "That little spitfire wanted to come with us. She wanted to get the hell out of Harvard and away from her daddy as much as we did."

"I didn't want to leave near as bad as you did," Rob said, matching his brother's glare.

"In case you didn't realize, little brother, we were the only white people in town. Hmmm?" He drew close to Rob's face and sniggered.

"Yeah, I noticed. And I also noticed they were some pretty nice folks."

"Nice folks? You think Hard Ivory's nice. Holy jumpin' lizards! That man almost killed me!"

"He was nice until he caught you poking his

daughter. That'd cause most men to lose their temper, Billy." Rob could see several small clusters of people staring their way.

"Yeah, I reckon you're right about that," Billy said with a laugh. "But as far as Pittsburg is concerned, you and everyone else knew we were leaving when I got my ribs healed. Now, they're healed, and here we are. Isn't that what you wanted?"

"No, that's not what I wanted," Rob yelled.

"Not what you wanted? Hey," Billy gave Rob a shove as he turned away, "don't turn your back on me while I'm talking. We stood right there in the middle of the yard and agreed to sell the farm. You were going with me and I was going to show you some of the places I've been. It was gonna be just you and me. What changed your mind?"

What changed my mind? Clara Jean suddenly appeared and Rob turned his head with a gulp.

"Oh, I get it. That skinny Russell girl. Hell, little brother, there's a lot better than her out there." He had no more than gotten the words out when Rob knocked him to the ground.

"Whoa, you must have it bad," Billy said, wiping blood from his lower lip against the back of his hand. "Okay, that's the way you want it? Let's see what you're made of." He scooted out of Rob's reach as he got to his feet.

"Don't you ever say anything like that again about Clara Jean," Rob hissed as Billy circled him.

"I won't have to."

Rob made several attempts to grab at him, only to have him dance out of his reach. Rob glanced at the crowd of people drawing closer, and Billy hit him with a hard right hand, followed by a left to the body and another right, knocking him to his knees.

"Had enough, little brother?" Billy stared down at Rob, kneeling and holding his side. He realized he had failed to move out of Rob's reach when his brother grabbed both boots and drove his shoulder against his knees.

Billy felt the air rush from his lungs as he hit the ground hard. Rob pounced on top and drove a hard fist into his face. Both brothers rolled across the ground punching and kicking. Rob was bigger and stronger, but Billy was quicker and a more cunning fighter. He slipped Rob's grip and danced to his feet. Rob made the mistake of springing after him and got several hard blows to the head for his effort. He wobbled on his feet after getting hit several more times, and was glad when two men rushed to separate them.

"Here, now. What the hell do you two think you're doing," one of them growled, tugging on Billy's collar.

"Easy, easy on the shirt, partner," Billy said, waving the man off. "I'm just trying to teach my little brother some manners."

"Brother? You're brothers?"

"Yeah, I'm Billy Mayfield, and that's my brother, Rob. We were having a family discussion that turned nasty, and I was giving him a different outlook on things."

"That right son?"

Rob blinked before the other man came into focus. "Yeah," he nodded, "that's what happened."

"Well, is it settled?"

"As far as I'm concerned. How about you, Rob? Is it finished?"

Rob nodded and spit, turning the leaves at his feet red.

"Okay, we'll leave you two to finish ironing things out, but don't kill one another." The man let go of Rob's arm and the two returned to the cluster gathered in the roadway.

"You okay," Billy asked, after the men were out of earshot.

"Yeah, I'm okay." Rob sniffed and held a hand to his nose. It was also bleeding.

"Come on. Let's take the horses to the creek and get washed up."

He grabbed the reins and followed his brother toward the sound of gurgling water. The thirsty animals lapped greedily and the cold water felt good against Rob's bruised face. But he knew he wasn't okay. He'd never be okay without Clara Jean. But, as he saw it, he didn't have any choice in the matter. Rob Mayfield was trapped. With the family farm gone, and their welcome at Douglass, Harvard and Pittsburg worn out, there was nothing left for him but to follow Billy, no matter where that road might take him.

Chapter 25

The next two days were spent in relative silence. One of the men who had helped break up the fight brought Billy and Rob plates of fried chicken and mashed potatoes for supper that evening. Rob had no trouble eating the mashed potatoes, but had to pick small pieces of chicken off the bone with his fingers due to his bruised and cut lips. They rested under the trees of Hamil's Chapel one more day, then left early the following morning, still traveling southwest, away from the cotton fields of Douglass and Pittsburg, away from Clara Jean, and in the opposite direction of New Orleans. Rob waited until they had reached Hainesville before broaching the subject again.

"Where are we headed, Billy? I may not have been there, but I know enough to know this ain't the way to New Orleans."

"No, it isn't, is it?" Billy grinned and sniggered as he pulled the saddle from his horse. They had stopped under a grove of cottonwoods growing on the bank of Mill Race Creek.

"You said we were going to New Orleans, but we're heading west. New Orleans is southeast."

"Yeah, I know where it is, and we're going. We're just taking a little detour, before heading toward New Orleans.

I've got a job to do first."

"What kind of a job?"

"I promise, nothing hard like picking cotton, little

brother." Billy laughed and slapped Rob on the shoulder. "A man south of here owes me some money, and I want to collect it before we head east. Really," he said as Rob gave him a skeptical look.

"How much money?" Rob pulled his own saddle from his horse and set it in a bed of leaves under one of the cottonwoods.

"Quite a bit, actually."

"Really." Rob paused in the middle of giving his horse a rubdown to stare at his brother. "How much is *quite a bit?*"

"Enough for me to wait until he sold a herd of cattle. That's why I didn't collect it before coming to get you." Billy perched himself on a fallen tree trunk and began rolling a cigarette.

"Why's this man owe you so much money?"

"Boy, little brother, you're just full of questions, aren't you?" Billy laughed as he fished a match from his shirt pocket and lit his smoke.

"Well, I'm finding it safer to ask questions when dealing with you, *big brother.*"

"Okay, no need to get puffed up about it," Billy said, and blew a cloud of smoke into the air. "We played cards and he lost the herd. Now he owes me money."

"You won a herd of cattle?" Rob dropped his bedroll and stared, as his brother nodded. "If you own a herd, why aren't you taking care of it?"

"*Owned* a herd. He's sold it by now, and it was too many cows for one man to take care of. Besides, I don't own a ranch to keep them on," he said with a grin.

"How many head are we talking about?" Rob was suddenly interested, and forgot about the bedroll as he listened.

"Oh, not a whole lot as Texas herds go. Five, maybe six hundred. Thing is," he continued as Rob whistled, "it was too many for me to handle by myself, and I don't own any land. Besides, cattle are a lot of work, and you know me, little brother, I ain't into doing a lot of work. So, I made a deal with Lester to keep his cows until they were full grown, then take them to market. Then we'd split the money after they were sold."

"What'll you get, half?"

"Half the money? After he's done all the work and paid his cowboys off? Naw, that wouldn't be right. I may be a lot of things, little brother, but I ain't greedy. Lester's going to give me a third and keep the rest." Billy crushed the butt under the toe of his boot and grinned. "That's why we're going to Cool Water before heading to New Orleans."

Rob sat on his heels thinking, as Billy pulled off his boots and dug around inside his saddle bags for his shining kit. Rob had known a few women around Douglass who spent time dressing and primping in front of a mirror, but he'd never known a man to spend half the time his brother did trying to look pretty. He waited until Billy was wiping the dust from his boots before speaking.

"I hate to tell you this, but Cold Water is to the north."

"I know," Billy glanced up and kept shining the black boots. "I didn't say, *Cold Water*. I said, *Cool Water*, and it lies southwest from here, not far from the Mexican border."

"The Mexican border?" Rob almost shouted. "The Mexican border's one heck've a long way from here. That one third you're getting had better be a lot of money. Besides, I've never heard of *Cool Water, Texas*."

"There's a lot of places you haven't heard of, little brother," Billy said with a laugh. "But most people haven't heard of Cool Water. It just kind of sprang up a couple of years ago, and isn't much of a town to start with...kind of like this town, Hainesville. What've we got here," he paused to stare toward the small community, "sixty or seventy people? Certainly no more than a hundred at the most, counting the blacks we saw living near the gristmill. They've only got one store and that little cafeteria we ate at. That's kind of what Cool Water's like, except it's got a livery, blacksmith shop and a bank."

"So, it's a little bigger than Hainesville?"

"Maybe, some…but not much." Billy finished one boot and started on the other. "Ol' Lester Bishop owns quite a spread south of Uvalde, and discovered the springs one day when he was buying cattle. They were bubbling right up out of the ground, with some of the sweetest tasting water you ever drank. Well, he buys a hunk of land, making sure the springs were just inside the boundary of his ranch, and decides to build a town to service the needs of his ranch. He made it sound like he was doing everybody a big favor, saying they wouldn't have to travel twenty or thirty miles to Carrizo Springs, unless they really wanted to. Thing is," he paused to grin at Rob, "seeing as he owns the town, he gets to keep the lion's share of the profits.

"Everything," Billy went on as he brought the second boot to a glassy shine, "he gets a share off the groceries, blacksmith shop, even the saloon. The old son-of-a-bitch goes to his own church every Sunday and listens to the preacher he hired, then collects his share from the whores working in his saloon. There," he held his boots in the fading sunlight and smiled.

"How'd you meet him?"

"Lester?"

"Yeah," Rob said with a nod.

"I got hired on as a hand on his ranch for awhile. I wasn't always lazy like you think, little brother. Anyway, ol' Lester used to come into the saloon on Saturday nights after he paid the hands. He'd drink and raise a little hell himself, just like the rest. Some of them thought he was just trying to be one of the boys, but not me. I got on the friendly side of

Ruth, his granddaughter, and she said he did it mostly to encourage the boys to spend their money, in order to recoup part of their pay." Billy set the boots aside and rolled another cigarette.

"Well, he comes in one Saturday, and decides he's gonna sit in on a friendly card game we've got going. We were just playing mostly for fun, you know...five cent ante...that sort of thing. Anyway, Lester decides he wants a little higher stakes, and starts raising 'em. Most of the boys didn't know how to play anymore than you do, so they folded right away. Well, I've got me a little poke and know something about cards, so I'm able to stay with him. Before you know it, things start getting serious, and Lester's losing his shirt. Most of the boys start telling me to quit while I'm ahead, but Lester won't let me." He paused to light his smoke.

"*Hell no, he's not leaving until I've got my money back*, he says and orders me to deal with a fresh deck. I tried telling him the deck wouldn't make any difference, but he wouldn't listen. So, I grabbed a new deck from the bartender, and broke it open. I even let him deal, and that didn't make much difference either. The old son-of-a-bitch didn't know beans about cards." Billy laughed and lay back on his blankets.

"Anyway, we kept on until he'd lost the eastern herd and threatened to shoot me. I quit and told him I'd come back and collect a third after he sold the cattle. So that, little brother, is why we're going to Cool Water."

"This isn't just another one of your stories, is it? The man does owe you the money," Rob said, as he made his own bed.

"One of my *stories*? Why, I'm shocked," Billy said with a laugh. "No, he owes me one third of the herd. I even had him put it into writing. Want to see the paper?"

"No, I believe you, if you say so."

"I hear a little skepticism in your voice, little brother."

"Well, wouldn't you be, after what we've been through?"

"All right, maybe I've made it a little hard on you, getting run out of Pittsburg the way I did, and you being all moonie over that girl. I'm sorry about that, Rob. I really am."

"I think you might actually mean that...maybe," Rob said, pulling his boots off.

"Well, I do. I'll tell you what," Billy leaned up on one elbow to look at his brother, "after we've collected my money from Lester and seen New Orleans, if you really want to go back to that Russell girl, you're welcome to go. I won't try talking you out of it."

"Really? You're not just saying that?"

"Nope, on my word of honor," Billy said with a raised hand.

"For whatever that's worth," Rob said with a laugh.

"Yeah, it might be a little shaky at that," Billy agreed, "I just wanted you to have more than we had growing up in Douglass. Hell, little brother, it's a big world out there. Look at the folks right here in Hainseville," he said pointing toward town. "Most of 'em will never see anything but their cotton or cane fields. Yeah, a couple of them might have a few peach trees, but that's all they'll ever know. I wanted you to see more than a cotton field. Maybe even eat a decent meal before dying." He leaned back and clasped his hands behind his head.

They lay silent for awhile, watching the setting sun through the leaves of the cottonwood trees. Rob had begun to think his brother might have dozed off when he again broke the silence.

"I know how you felt about the girl and I'm truly sorry, Rob. I've never felt that way about any woman I can remember. I might never really fall in love. Who knows how the cards are going to be dealt? Thing is, if you'd have stayed with the Russells, the only thing you would have seen was their little farm. Maybe you would have gotten married, built a house on the other side of the field, raised a bunch of kids and cotton. That's all. But, if that's what you really want out of life, you're welcome to it. Only come help me collect my money and see New Orleans. After that, you're free to go, and no hard feelings. By then, everyone will have forgotten about me shooting Harry Lippert, and welcome you back with opened arms."

"Help you collect your money? Why do I need to help you collect your money if you have it written on a piece of paper?"

"Because, little brother, remember me saying that I'd gotten on the friendly-side of Lester's granddaughter?"

"Uh-huh." Rob rolled over to look at his brother. He was lying back and grinning.

"Well…I was on the *friendly-side* of Ruth, and he caught us in the hayloft. I had to leave in kind of a hurry," Billy said with a laugh.

"Dear Jesus in heaven, what have I gotten myself into?" Rob moaned as he laid back and closed his eyes.

Chapter 26

New Hope, in Collin County, was a community of less than a hundred people, counting the children. Billy remarked to the man who ran the small grocery store they ought to start counting the dogs and chickens, so they could top a hundred.

"Maybe so," he said, adding the figures on a pad of paper. "That'll be five cents for the bacon, another five for the rolling tobacco and papers, a dollar for the whiskey, ten cents for the flour. That comes to a total of one dollar and twenty cents."

"Here, buy yourself a cigar," Billy said, tossing two dollars on the counter.

"Why, thank you, sir. I think I will." He tossed the coins into the money box and pulled a cigar from a jar. He was a small man, with leathery skin and gray beard and hair. "Those are pretty fancy duds to be traveling by horseback in," he said, eying Billy up and down.

"Yeah, but you never know who you might run into out there. Besides, I like to impress the coyotes and jackrabbits."

The man laughed and lit his cigar. Billy leaned in the open doorway and studied the empty street separating the few weathered buildings. He could see a church that doubled as a schoolhouse, a blacksmith shop and a grange hall, but little else, except the general store he was standing in. If it hadn't been for the dog lying in the sun next to the door, the clanging sound coming from the blacksmith shop and Rob watering the horses at a trough, one might have thought the town deserted.

"What do you folks do for excitement around here?" Billy gave the man a sideways glance.

"Excitement?" He walked to stand next to Billy.

"Yeah, you know. What do you do to blow off some steam? I don't see any saloon, or dance hall."

"That's because there aren't any." He paused to knock the ashes from the cigar. "The folks who built New Hope did it mainly as a school and church community for the area farmers. They were religious people, and weren't looking to blow off any steam. To them, a good sermon on Sunday mornings is excitement enough."

"And what do you think?" Billy gave him a sideways glance.

"Me? I think whatever they believe is fine with me, as long as they keep buying their supplies inside my store."

"You mean you're not one of them?" Billy shifted to study the man.

"No, I didn't say that. What I said was, whatever they want to believe is fine with me. I'm as much a part of this community as I need to be. I run the store, mind my own business and let folks be. In turn, they buy what things they can't grow and let me be. We get along just fine."

"Hmm," Billy snorted, "guess that makes you a little different than most folks I've run into. Seems everyone nowadays wants to know another man's business."

"I'll tell you what it makes me. It makes me smart," he said with a nod. "You see," he pointed at Billy with the cigar, "suppose you came in here with a past, and didn't want folks knowing who you were, or where you're going. Then, suppose someone came looking for you a couple of days later.

All I could tell them was, a couple of fellas bought some grub, but I don't know who they were, and I don't know where they went. I can't even recall what they really looked like. That way, I don't have to worry about anyone coming back to settle a score, and next time you were in the area, you'd know where to buy your supplies." He grinned and took a puff off the cigar.

"You think I'm on the run?" Billy eyed the man carefully.

"No sir, I personally don't. If you was, you wouldn't be dressed that away, drawing attention to yourself. I'm just saying everyone's got a past. Some folks may not mind sharing their past, but others do."

"What about you? Do you have a past?"

"Like I said, everyone's got a past. Mine? I come here ten years ago, looking for a place to lick my wounds. Folks took me in and didn't ask questions. I figure some of them might've had things they didn't want to think about. The war had a way of doing that to folks, you know. Anyway, I opened this store and began treating these folks the way they treated me, and we get along just fine."

"By the way, my name's Billy Mayfield. That's my brother, Rob, watering the horses."

"Folks just call me George."

He took another puff from the cigar without offering his hand during the introduction. It wasn't hard for Billy to imagine what the store clerk might have been, prior to arriving in New Hope. Most clerks he'd known were fair-skinned, and well-bred. But this wiry, leather-skinned, bow-legged little man was none of those things. He'd met such men in his travels, and figured the lines in this man's face were maps leading to things better left forgotten.

"Like I said, Billy Mayfield, I didn't think you were trying to hide your tracks, or you wouldn't be dressed that away. But as far as I'm concerned, I leave people be, and they leave me be. They buy my goods and I take their money. We get along just fine."

"Smart way to be," Billy said thoughtfully. "Ever just want to let the wolf out?"

"What makes you ask that?" George eyed Billy up and down.

"No reason. I don't see a saloon or gambling hall."

"You won't, either. Some of these folks may have a past, but they're religious. Only liquor you'll see around New Hope is inside my store. I sell it for snakebites."

"Anyone ever get snake-bitten around here?"

"Oh, almost every day," George said with a snort. "Hell of a lot of snakes in New Hope. I get bit once or twice a day myself. Which reminds me..." He pulled a flask from his hip pocket and took a swig, before passing it to Billy.

"Thanks," Billy said, passing the flask back to its owner.

"Yeah, I let the wolf loose about once a month when I go to Tyler for supplies. It's only twenty-five miles or so, and I could make the trip in a couple of days in my wagon. But I take four or five days, 'cause I know a widow woman there, who likes howling at the moon as much as I do. I figure some of these folks got a suspicion what I do, but they've never mentioned it. They leave me alone, and I leave them alone." He took another pull from his flask and passed it to Billy, then stood on the porch next to the sleeping dog and stared at the empty street. Rob was returning with the horses.

"Yep, these are some great folks. Drought's been tough on them," George said thoughtfully. "A lot of them have lost nearly everything. Several families have packed up and moved back east, and I hear folks all over Texas are fixin' to do the same. Guess they weren't cut out for pioneering."

"Reckon not." Billy passed the flask back to George and joined him on the porch. "Don't reckon I was either. Cards might be a risky way to earn a dollar, but they are a whole like easier on your back than a mule and a plow."

"You got that right." George laughed and toasted him with the flask.

Rob led the horses up to where the men were standing and eyed the two sharing the flask before speaking. "Well, we leaving or staying?"

"I thought we might spend the night, but it doesn't look like there's any place to hang our hats. I guess we'll camp on the road tonight," Billy said.

"You two are welcome to spend the night at my house, if you don't mind sleeping on the floor with Hank," George said.

"Whose Hank," Rob asked.

"Hank's my dog," George said, nudging the hound with his toe. The dog opened one eye without moving. "He doesn't mind sharing his fleas with company."

"No, thanks," Billy said, grabbing his saddlebags. "I'm getting sort of used to sleeping in the open. We'll camp four or five miles down the road." He tied the bags on the horse before clasping the storekeeper by the shoulder.

"Thanks for the drink, and you take it easy, old timer."

"You too, the both of you."

"We aim to do just that."

Billy mounted his bay and gave one final wave, before nudging the horse into a gentle lope. He passed the blacksmith shop and turned directly south toward Tyler, with Rob following.

Chapter 27

"Yeah, they were here." The coverall-clad man leaned heavily against his hoe and nodded. He had been weeding his garden when the men on horseback approached and began asking questions. They were three of the ugliest men he remembered seeing.

"Are they still here?" The larger one of the three leaned in his saddle, causing the leather to squeak. He had a crooked nose and several missing teeth. The remaining teeth were tobacco-stained and rotten.

"No sir. They were camped a couple of days under that clump of trees near the creek. Right over yonder by the church." He pointed with the hoe.

"And how long ago was that," the man asked.

"Mmmm, maybe a week ago. They was here only a couple of days, then left. Why you looking for them, may I ask? Y'all kin?"

"You might say that. We're looking for them 'cause cousin Harry died, and we thought they might like to know. I'm Vernon Lippert, and these are my brothers, Al and Gene." The men nodded as they were introduced. They were almost as ugly as their brother, and certainly didn't look to be cut from the same cloth as the Mayfield brothers. But every family he knew had undesirable relatives. Walter Fraiser shrugged his shoulders.

"Aw, that's too bad. I hope you catch up with them."

"So do we, mister. Did they say where they were going? We'd sure like to give them the news."

"No sir. Can't say they talked to folks much. Just kinda stayed to themselves and licked their wounds."

"Wounds?" The Lippert brothers glanced at each other.

"Yes sir. Had a heck of a row when they first got here. Liked to beat the stuffin's outa each other. Especially the younger one. His face was still black and blue when they pulled out."

"Yeah, that sounds like cousin Billy," Vernon Lippert said as the three men burst into laughter. "Wouldn't have any idée what they was fussing 'bout, would you?"

"No. Someone said they mentioned a girl, but I don't know for sure."

The men laughed even harder.

"Yeah, that's Billy alright. Much obliged."

"Walt."

"Say what?" Vernon started to turn his horse but paused.

"Said my name was Walt. Walter Fraiser."

"Well, Walt, you've been a big help. Y'all wouldn't mind us spending the night under those trees, would you?"

"No sir. God made 'em, so I reckon they belong to everyone. Oh, one more thing," he added as they turned their horses.

"Yeah, what might that be?"

"They headed down that road when they left." He pointed with the hoe. "Heads southeast from here towards New Hope. Thought you might like to know, since you're looking for them."

"Much obliged Walt. We'll let you get back to your hoeing now." The Lippert brothers walked their horses toward the clump of trees in silence.

They had spent the day following the funeral with their ailing mother and Harry's widow, and the decision had cost them dearly. They found the trail outside of Pittsburg surprisingly cold, and the following two days were spent asking questions. A gambler dressed like Bill Mayfield shouldn't have been that hard to find, but few people remembered seeing him. The going had been slow, but Vernon felt they had received their first real clue since leaving home. He grinned as he heaved his saddle and bedroll onto a pile of leaves under a tree. New Hope. Perhaps the name had a double meaning. They would head that way in the morning and see if Billy Mayfield was there.

Chapter 28

Tyler, Texas, with its bustling population of five thousand, was the exact opposite of New Hope. Rob had never seen so many people packed into one place, and was taken aback when people either walked or drove their wagons and buggies carelessly in front of him, causing him to rein his horse to a halt. Only a handful of people seemed to notice when two men pushed their way out of a saloon and began pounding on each other in the middle of the street. Rob followed Billy, who guided his horse around the two combatants, and went on as if they were invisible. According to the gruff man at the livery, they were lucky to catch him at the right time. Two men had left with their horses an hour earlier, and he had just enough room to stable their animals for a few days.

"Well, what do you think, little brother," Billy asked as they stepped out into the busy street.

"I don't rightly know. I've never seen a place like this," Rob said, as he stared wide-eyed.

"Sure different than Douglass, that's for certain. Wait until we get to Austin and San Antonio."

"Why, are they bigger?"

"Maybe, a might," Billy said, eying Rob up and down. "There's places even bigger than they are. Thing is, little brother, we've got to get you some new clothes. You stand out like a cotton farmer, that's for sure."

"I reckon that's what I am, Billy," Rob said with a snigger.

"Not anymore, little brother. Not anymore." He slapped Rob on the shoulder and guided him down the street.

His brother spent what Rob considered a small fortune buying him two pair of corduroy pants, two shirts, a pair of riding boots, wide-brimmed hat, and a .44 caliber Smith and Wesson with belt and holster.

"What do I need a handgun for? I ain't never shot one before," Rob protested when his brother handed him the weapon.

"I'll teach you. Besides, you might be thanking me some day. Now, let's find us a room and get something to eat. My stomach's beginning to think my throat's been cut."

They checked into a small boarding house located about two blocks from the livery just before supper. The owner, an attractive widow in her mid-forties named Wanda Johnson, made the boys remove their guns before entering the dining room.

"It wouldn't make me any difference if you were Wyatt Earp, everyone has to check their hardware before sitting at my table, and that goes for spurs," she said, giving their boots a quick glance. "I'm tired of having my furniture gouged and scratched up by men too lazy to remove their spurs."

"And rightfully so, Ma'am," Billy said with a grin as he unbuckled his gunbelt. "Our ma used to pitch a fit if one of us saddled up to her table with guns and spurs. Didn't she, Rob?"

"Uh-huh," Rob agreed with a nod, knowing it was another of Billy's bold-faced lies. Billy was the only Mayfield that ever carried a pistol, and there was no need for spurs while working a cotton field.

"I must say, these are some of the fanciest guns and spurs I've ever seen." Wanda eyed Billy's pearl-handled pistols and silver spurs before locking them in a closet. "Where ya'll hail from anyway?"

"Hail from? Why we are native Texicans, Ma'am," Billy said with pride. Rob agreed whole-heartedly, knowing he was at long-last telling the truth about something.

After an honest-to-god home-cooked meal of fried chicken, mashed potatoes, gravy and green beans, they spent a pleasant evening sitting in the parlor and listening to a skinny redheaded girl who was staying at the boarding house play an old upright piano, who Rob later discovered to be a niece of Wanda's. He was surprised his brother had decided to stay in the parlor, instead of finding a good poker game somewhere. He was even more than surprised when Billy became involved in a friendly game of bridge with Wanda and several guests. Two old men tried several times to get Rob interested in a game of checkers, but he declined as he sipped a cup of hot tea, pretending to listen to the redheaded girl torture the piano keys. He was most interested in watching his brother.

Rob decided, as the evening wore on, the girl wasn't a half-bad piano player, compared to those he had heard around Douglass, but had to squint his eyes when she sang and hit the high notes. Billy, on the other hand, never flinched during the recital, and seemed content to play bridge with Wanda and her guests. After listening for an hour to ear-splitting tunes, Rob excused himself and went to bed. He rose early the next morning to visit the outhouse, and discovered Billy slipping quietly from Wanda's bedroom, carrying his shiny boots in his hand.

Chapter 29

Billy spent the following week between the Trail Dust Saloon, a mid-sized place within walking distance from the boarding house, and keeping Wanda Johnson happy. He was down to his last twenty-dollar gold piece after buying Rob's clothes and paying for their room, and the poker table was the quickest and easiest way he knew of to grow a bankroll. Rob, on the other hand, had taken a job at the livery against his wishes.

"What the hell are you trying to do, ruin our image?"

"What image?" The blank look on Rob's face reminded Billy of a calf staring at a new gate.

"The image I've been busting my butt to create, you idgit! I buy you new clothes, a gun and a hat, and you take to the livery and start mucking out stalls."

"Well…," Rob drug the word like it was hogtied, "a man's gotta earn a living."

"That's what I've been doing the last few days. Look," he said, tossing a roll of bills on the bed, "that's what I've been doing, and it's a whole lot cleaner and easier than shoveling horseshit and ruining your new clothes. Look at your boots! Go on, look at them."

"Well…" Rob said, staring at the scuffed boots, "they would've gotten like that if we were punching cows."

"Yeah, and I'll admit that's better'n hoeing cotton, or mucking stalls, but we're not punching cattle. We're not going to work like that ever again." Billy dug through his bags and tossed Rob a can of boot wax.

"Here, clean 'em up and make yourself presentable."

"Okay, but what do you plan on us doing, if we're not going to work, Billy? I get mighty hungry when I don't eat," Rob raised his voice as he removed his boots.

"You've been eating, haven't you? I ain't let either one of us go hungry yet, have I?"

"No, but you know as well as I do that cards are a risky business at best. What if you have a run of bad luck someday? Wouldn't it be good if we had something to fall back on? Say, like my job at the stable?" Rob began vigorously brushing the dirt from his boots.

"Don't you worry about having something to fall back on. I've already taken care of that."

"Yeah, what?"

"Just don't you worry about what. I've got it covered. You worry about getting yourself presentable for dinner," Billy said as he opened the door.

"And what am I supposed to do while you're playing cards and seeing the landlady?" Rob glared at him as he snapped the can of boot wax open.

"Oh, I don't know, you'll think of something," Billy said with a shrug, as the redheaded girl giggled downstairs. "How about keeping her company for awhile. She ain't half-bad looking."

Billy laughed and closed the door as his brother growled and threw the polishing rag. Rob had a lot of rough edges and might take some work, but Billy was sure he could eventually turn him into something presentable, given the time. He paused at the bottom of the stairs as Wanda appeared.

"Now, where are you off to?"

"I'm off to work, my dear. A man's got to earn a living, doesn't he?" He finished by giving her a quick kiss.

"Not here...not now," she said pushing him away. "Someone might see us!"

"And what if they do? I've never made it any secret how I feel about you. Everyone knows I'm in love with you."

"Yes, but Margaret..." Billy pulled her close and kissed her again, cutting her off.

"That little redhead is so taken with my kid brother, she wouldn't notice if we were both standing here naked."

"Billy!" She blushed and tried prying herself loose as he gave her another kiss. He liked the color in her cheeks and decided to make her blush more often.

"It's true and you know it."

"Yes, but..."

He drew her body tightly against his and kissed her passionately. Wanda pulled away gasping for breath.

"Keep that thought in mind. I'll be home early tonight." He slipped his hat on, and gave the brim a final adjustment with a grin.

He spied a blushing Margaret Yarbrough in the dining room as he passed. The girl had evidently seen and heard the exchange of affection by the stairs. *Maybe she's primed enough to go make a man out of Rob.* The thought caused him to chuckle as he walked briskly toward the Trail Dust. He actually liked Wanda, in an odd sort of way. She was attractive, for a woman twice his age, and certainly had plenty of fire in her veins. She was also comfortable with herself as a lover, and knew things about keeping a man happy that never crossed a younger woman's mind. Their relationship might be able to grow given the chance, but not into something serious. In another ten years he would be reaching his prime, while Wanda would begin to show her age. He paused to light a cigarette.

Wanda Johnson was someone to fall back on if his luck at the card table did happen to turn. As long as he kept her happy inside the bedroom, she would keep a roof over their heads and food in their stomachs. He might even be able to weasel a few dollars out of her now and again for a stake at the table. The one thing he hadn't told her was, he'd be packing in a few days to take care of some unfinished business in Cool Water. In the meantime, he reasoned again, he did sort of like her, and a man needed a woman to keep him warm in the evenings, even if that woman happened to be Wanda Johnson.

Chapter 30

They had been in Tyler for two weeks when Billy's luck turned bad. He was seated in the same chair at the same table inside the Trail Dust, but this night things were somehow different. Across the table was a man he'd never seen before, dressed in tattered coveralls, trail-worn boots and sweat-stained hat. His appearance wouldn't impress anyone as the man being a gambler, but Billy had never seen a slicker card shark inside any of the saloons and card rooms he'd been in. The five-hundred-dollar bankroll he had won at that very table was down to a few dollars. He would have quit long ago, except for the fact that he knew the man was cheating, but Billy couldn't see how.

"I'll see your two dollars, and raise you ten," the man in coveralls said with a grin.

"Well, I'll tell you what, my friend, you can have the two dollars, because I'm out," Billy said, tossing his cards to the center of the table.

"What's the matter, Sonny, you need to borrow a few dollars?" Jake, who was seated to his left, laughed. Billy had known him as a bad loser the few times he had played against him, and wanted to smash the man in the mouth, but smiled instead.

"No, thank you. I've got money back in my room, but it's getting late," he bounced a twenty-dollar gold piece in his palm, "and I certainly don't have enough to stay in this game." He leaned back as a scantily-clad girl approached the table.

"Excuse me, Angel, could you bring a bottle and fresh glasses for my friends? And," he paused as he placed the coin in her hand, "keep the change, darlin'."

"Why, thank you, Billy. What about a glass for you? Ain't you staying?"

"No," he shook his head, "I'll just finish this glass. I'm afraid I had a run of bad luck tonight, and I'm broke. I don't even have enough money to come visit you."

"You've never come to visit me, Billy, in all the times
I've asked you."

"That's true, isn't it," Billy said as the men at the table laughed. "Well, I'll tell you what, Angel, I'll come see you tomorrow. Now, what about that bottle and glasses?"

"Okay, but I'm holding you to your promise. Tomorrow...okay?"

"Yes, I promise, tomorrow." He kissed her hand and the girl swished away smiling.

"Well, whadda ya know? Maybe you'll get lucky after all," Jake said with a laugh. "Come back after you've seen Angel, and let's see if it helps your card-playing."

"No, I don't need to see a flea-bitten whore to improve my game," Billy said as he scooted away from the table. "I'm always lucky, Jake, you just don't know how lucky yet." He lifted his half-full glass from the table in a toast.

"Well, gentlemen, it has been a pleasure." He downed the rest of his drink and set the glass back on the table with a flare. "Good evening."

Billy could hear the man in coveralls as he headed toward the door. "That boy's shore got class, if nothing else."

He walked to the corner of the building where he paused to roll and light a cigarette. Then, when he thought no one was looking, he slipped around the corner and hurried toward the rear of the Trail Dust, where the outhouses were located. Everyone inside the saloon would eventually have to visit the back of the building, and most, especially after a few drinks, simply pee'd in the alley, instead of trying to find their way around a dirty outhouse in the dark. The bottle he had purchased as a goodwill gesture would soon take effect. Now all he had to do was wait.

Billy stood in the shadows smoking and watching. Several men made their way out the rear door and relieved themselves against the side of the saloon, then staggered back inside. Billy finished his smoke and waited some more. He had begun to roll another cigarette when the rear door swung open and Jake staggered into the alley in a beam of yellow, followed by the coverall-clad man. They were both intoxicated and laughing, and Jake had to lean against the side of the building in order to make water. Billy tossed his makings aside and removed the leather thongs from both pistols as he crept up behind them.

"Good evening, gentlemen," Billy said, shoving a muzzle to the back of both men's heads and cocking the hammers.

"Ohmygod, Billy! Please don't kill me!" Jake begged.

"Easy, boy," the one in coveralls said, raising both hands. "Don't do nothing stupid. We was just having a little fun in there."

"I want to know one thing," Billy said. "How'd you do it?"

"I beg your pardon?" The coverall man was cool. Billy had to give him credit. Jake on the other hand, had pee'd down his trouser legs.

"Take it easy, Jake." Billy gave him a rap with the gun. "I'd hate to splatter what little brains you have all over the side of the building. Now, maybe you can tell me," he prodded the coverall man with the gun, "how'd you do it? I know you were cheating, but I sat there all evening and still couldn't figure it out."

"I wasn't cheating, Billy. Whatever gave you that idea?"

"You want to see Jesus being a lying card cheat? I'm a pretty good poker player, and I've sat with some of the best. I know their tricks, but I've never seen anyone like you. Now, you tell me, before I lose what little patience I have left. What were you doing in there?"

"Okay, I don't blame you for getting sore. My name's William La Rogue. I used to work on a riverboat on the Mississippi. People called me Diamond Bill. I've known Jake Billings a long time, and just happened to be in town. He told me you were a card cheat, and had taken a lot of his money. He asked me to sit in on the game tonight and win some of it back."

"You said that?" Billy prodded Jake with the gun. "You called me a cheat? I killed a man in Cookville for that very thing."

"Oh, please, Billy! My God man, please don't kill me!" Jake fell to his knees begging.

"Jesus, man, have some pride." He gave Jake a shove with is foot, and the man toppled over backward into a puddle of urine. "At least die with a little dignity." Diamond Bill started to move, but Billy shoved the gun against the back of his neck.

"No need killing us, Billy. I watched you real close tonight, and I told Jake I didn't think you'd been cheating anyone. He's a lousy card player in the first place, and I think you're better'n him."

"Yeah, you think so? Well, that doesn't help much does it? You've still got my money, and you did it by cheating. Now, I'll give you exactly thirty seconds to tell me how, or I'll send you to Jesus being a cheat and a liar."

"I knew you were too good to do a bottom-deal,

'cause you'd spot that right away. So, I used signals."

"Signals?"

"Yeah," he said with a nod. "You didn't notice how Angel kept passing our table every few minutes? I slipped her a few dollars before the game, and it was her job to look at your cards, and tell me what you were holding. Honest…that's how we did it. I used a girl that way on the riverboats."

"Jesus," Billy said with a laugh, shaking his head. "Angel sure won't get to heaven doing that sort of thing. The next question is, what I do with you two?" He backed away as Diamond Bill turned slowly to face him. Jake was still lying in the urine, crying.

"Well, there's no need for anything like that," Diamond Bill said with a weak laugh. "Here," he held one hand in the air and reached into his coveralls, "you can have your money back." He pushed a wad on money toward Billy. "Take it…go ahead."

Billy holstered his left gun and shoved the crumpled wad of bills into his pocket.

"There, now we're even," Diamond Bill said with a sick laugh.

"Almost," Billy said, and slammed the gun over the man's head. Diamond Bill crumpled to the ground with a groan. Billy holstered the pistol and straightened his vest.

"You're getting off easy, mister. We either shoot or hang most four-flushers in Texas."

He had almost reached the corner of the building when he heard Jake's voice behind him.

"You son-of-a-bitch!"

Billy glanced over his shoulder as the drunken man pointed a gun at him. Billy whipped his left pistol upward as the man fired. Jake's bullet slammed harmlessly into one of the outhouses as Billy's fired. His bullet tore through the drunken man's chest. Jake slumped back into the puddle of urine he had been lying in, dead.

Billy quickly turned the corner as excited voices came from the alley behind the saloon. The place would be crawling with people and lawmen in a matter minutes. Without a witness, he'd be sunk, and there was no telling what Diamond Bill would say, once he came to. He paused in the darkness and stuffed the wad of bills inside one of his boots. He then ejected the spent cartridge from his pistol and replaced it with the one he carried in his pocket for that very purpose. Anyone checking his guns would find them loaded, and all the cartridge loops on his belt filled.

He straightened his clothing and entered the busy street, calmly smoking a cigarette. He glanced over his shoulder at the noisy crowd rushing to and from the saloon, and even asked a man what all the excitement was about. He then strolled at a brisk pace toward the boardinghouse. The ruse would only work for perhaps a half hour, maybe an hour at the most. Then, when Diamond Bill regained his senses, he would tell what happened and they would put two and two together. It would only be a matter of time, before they came to the boardinghouse looking for him. He was going to have to break the news to Rob that their welcome in Tyler had just worn out. Billy tossed the cigarette into the street, wondering what kind of a fit Wanda was going to pitch when she found them gone.

Chapter 31

"Is that the truth?"

"Is what the truth?"

"What you said about killing that man, and us having to sneak out of Tyler in the middle of the night."

"Oh Christ Almighty!"

They had been riding in silence for almost four hours, heading south toward Jacksonville. Billy had been surprised how Wanda Johnson had taken the news. She was leaving the kitchen with a hot cup of tea when he entered the front door, and smiled when she realized he was home early. Of course, she believed it was in order to keep his promise of a romantic night in her bed. Not wanting to waste more time than necessary, he took her by the arm and led her back into the kitchen, where he explained truthfully what had happened. Instead of screaming and pitching the fit he half expected, Wanda sat quietly sipping her tea, then calmly placed the cup on the table and kissed him.

"You'd better wake your brother and get busy packing. Most anyone who knows you, knows you're staying here. I'll send Margaret after your horses."

Margaret Yarbrough, on the other hand, did pitch a fit like Billy had never seen. She cried and wailed and clung to Rob like a young bride watching her husband go to war. Rob had to pry himself loose in order to mount his horse. Billy was half-disappointed that Wanda hadn't taken on so over him, seeing as he had slept with her, and Rob hadn't given more than polite conversation at the dinner table to Margaret.

It wasn't until he was giving the saddle cinches one final tug, that she slipped up from behind him and kissed his ear.

"You come back to see me when this all dies down, now you hear," she said, kissing his neck and mapping his body with her hands.

"Yeah, I certainly will." Billy took Wanda in his arms and kissed her repeatedly. "I'll write you and let you know when I'm settled. You can either come to me, or tell me when it's safe to return to Tyler."

"Whichever you wish, Darling." She kissed him again. "Now go, before someone sees you."

Billy mounted his horse, and they left.

For once, Billy found himself meaning every word. He liked Wanda, and discovered he was going to miss her. She was attractive and comfortable to be around. He could not remember, as he rode away, Wanda ever being clingy or saying anything silly and embarrassing like the younger women he had been with. Wanda Johnson was a lady, perhaps the only real lady he had kept company with, and he like being with her. He had been busy deciding how he would include her in his plans, when Rob started asking what he considered stupid questions.

"Yes, it's the truth, every word of it. Why?"

"Why?" Rob drew his horse close and scowled. "Lord Almighty, big brother! You've never done nothing but tell lies and half-truths since we started. Why should I believe you?"

"Now that, little brother, is a bold-faced lie. I've always told you the truth."

"Huh, not likely. You've just made yourself out to be a bigger liar." Rob allowed his horse to drift back to a comfortable distance as they continued following the road. The countryside took on an orange glow as the sun broke the Texas sky.

"Nope, you're wrong again, little brother. I've never

hidden anything from you, because I don't have anything to hide."

"You've gotten us run out of every town we've been in!"

"That may be true," Billy laughed, "but I didn't lie about it. Look," he shifted in the saddle to stare at his angry brother, "you were there when Hank came at me with the shotgun. I could've killed him, but I didn't. It was the same with that guy back in Cookville."

"You bashed his head in, Billy. I was there and saw it."

"Yeah, and if you remember, he was the one who started it."

"What about Pittsburg, huh? You killed a man and got us run out of there too!"

"Again for the same reason. He had a gun pointed at me, and was fixing to pull the trigger. Boy," Billy laughed, "leaving Pittsburg's still a sore spot for you, isn't it?"

Rob didn't answer and kept his attention focused on the road ahead.

"Well, I'll tell you what," Billy said, shifting back in the saddle, "if it makes you feel any better, I felt pretty much the same leaving Tyler."

"Huh?" Rob turned to stare.

"I said, I didn't want to leave Wanda any more than you wanted to leave that skinny farm girl."

"Clara Jean Russell wasn't a *skinny farm girl!*"

"Whoa, easy little brother. I didn't mean any harm. I know how you feel about her, and said you can go back and pick cotton, get married and raise a big family to your heart's content after we square things in Cool Water. I'm just saying I sort of felt the same thing leaving Wanda Johnson."

"She's older than you, Billy."

"Yeah, some, as far as years go, but she felt good, like a broken-in saddle, or a good pair of boots. I don't know. It's hard to explain, and doesn't really matter none, does it?"

They rode in silence for the next few minutes before Rob again broke the silence.

"You love her?"

"Who?"

"The landlady, Wanda Johnson."

"Love? I don't know. I liked being with her, and age didn't seem to matter. Why?"

"No reason. Just wondering."

They were approaching Jacksonville when Billy turned off the road toward a large house with red curtains hanging in the window. A young woman was standing on the porch in her unmentionables smoking a cigarette.

"Jesus, Billy what kind of place is this?"

"Right now, it's a place to get a hot bath, something to eat and some sleep. Anything else you might get is entirely up to you, little brother."

Chapter 32

The first day was spent doing what Billy had said. He made arrangements with an attractive woman Rob guessed to be in her thirties, for two rooms, hot baths, and a hot meal.

"Well, that's an unusual request," the woman said with a laugh. "Men looking for that sort of thing usually check into the hotel in town, not here."

"I realize that, ma'am, but we've been riding all night, and to tell the truth," Billy drew close, "I had a little trouble in Tyler, and would rather stay out of sight for a couple of days."

"Ah, I see." She nodded and rapped her long fingernails against the table next to her chair. "I guess we might be able to accommodate you, as long as there's no trouble. I don't want any of my girls hurt, understand?"

Both men nodded.

"If the law comes here looking for you, you're on your own, and I'll kill you myself if one of my girls gets hurt. Is that plain enough?"

"Ma'am," Billy gave the woman one of his best smiles, "I'm a native born Texican. I wouldn't stand for anyone hurting one of these lovely ladies myself." He finished by gesturing toward the several scantily-clad women eying the two brothers.

"Good, we understand each other. That'll be forty dollars a day for the both of you."

"What?" Billy acted surprised.

"You said you wanted room and board, didn't you? If

that's too rich for your blood, try the hotel in town."

"No, ma'am, I didn't mean it that away," Billy said shaking his head. "I thought you would charge much more than twenty dollars apiece, especially when the ladies are so darned beautiful."

"Huh, they are pretty, but you're full of it, I'll tell you that," the woman said with a snort as the girls giggled.

"Maybe I am full of horse manure, but I meant every word of it. I'll tell you what," Billy dug inside the top of his left boot and pulled out a wad of money, "I'm giving you a hundred dollars to start out with, and we'll settle-up when we leave."

"Well, I see that you and I will get along just fine," she said with a grin, then turned toward the girls and began barking orders.

"Lois, you take their horses to the stable, and tell George to hide their saddles. Lavender, why don't you and Alice fetch some hot water and see these gentlemen receive a relaxing bath?" She turned back toward Billy as the girls began to scramble. "By the way, I'm Lola. Welcome to my palace."

******

Rob had a hard time undressing in front of the girl named Alice, and even harder time allowing her to give him a bath. He was certain God would send a bolt of lightning to strike him dead any second.

"You've never done anything like this before, have you honey?" He could feel her hot breath against his ear as she leaned to wash his chest. The hand holding the washcloth inched its way lower and Rob grabbed her wrist.

"No, I haven't."

"Well, no need to be scared, darlin', I don't bite none…not much anyway, and it's all in fun when I do. Just relax and enjoy your bath." She poured a pan-full of warm water over his head.

"Ever have a girlfriend?"

"Yes, ma'am."

"Did you ever do anything more'n just talk?" She began massaging Rob's scalp and neck.

"Yes, ma'am. Me and Clara Jean love each other a whole lot."

"Oh, why don't you tell me about her? Is she pretty?"

Her fingers felt good against his sore muscles and he closed his eyes as he talked about Clara Jean. He had no idea when he dozed off, but the bathwater felt cool against his skin, as her lips and silky voice against his ear woke him.

"Better wake up, darlin', Lola says the cook has your breakfast ready, and you don't want your eggs cold, do you?"

******

It was late in the afternoon when he was awakened by someone crawling into the bed next to him. Rob froze as an arm snaked its way across his chest and a warm body nuzzled against his back.

"You must've been plum tuckered out, darlin', 'cause you've been asleep nearly ten hours. Feeling better?" Her lips and hot breath against his ear caused his body to react in strange ways.

"Yes, ma'am."

"Yes what?" Her lips inched down his neck. He discovered she did bite, but not hard, and it didn't hurt at all. It caused him to tremble.

"Yes, I feel better."

"Good." Her hands moved under his undershirt and caressed his chest, causing the shirt to hike up in back.

"Good Lord," he said as her breasts pressed against his back. "You're naked, ma'am."

"I certainly am," she giggled, "and you oughta be too. Here," she grabbed the undershirt and jerked it upward and tugged it over his head. "There, that's better. Now," she lay on top of him and continued nibbling his neck as she talked. "Little ol' Alice is gonna take you to wonderland."

"Where, ma'am?" He was finding it hard to breathe, but not from her weight.

"Wonderland...like in Lewis Carroll's book, you know...*Alice's Adventures In Wonderland*? Only the adventures I'm gonna take you on are much better."

"Oh," Rob said, only he'd never heard of Lewis Carroll, much less read his book. He caught his breath as the girl's lips and hands moved toward places he'd never dreamed of.

"No...no! I'm sorry, ma'am. I just can't," he said, rolling her onto the bed and holding her at arm's length.

"Why, are you scared of little ol' Alice," she said with a giggle. "I won't hurt you."

"No, it ain't that, ma'am."

"Then what?" She moved one of his hands toward her breast and he pulled it away.

"I...I'm gonna get married."

"So? I've got lots of married men who come and visit me. Being married doesn't bother them."

"Maybe, but it would me. It ain't you, honest. You're possibly the prettiest girl I've seen, and seeing you sitting there," he gestured toward her nude body, "in my bed, really makes be wanna do those things. But I promised Clara Jean she'd be the only woman I'd...do those things with."

"You're not kidding, are you?"

"No, ma'am."

"Wow," she said, shaking her head slowly. "I wish someone loved me like that. Wanna tell me about her?"

"Sure. Only we'd better cover you some." Rob pulled the blanket around her shoulders and across her breasts. "I might get tempted to enter your wonderland."

Chapter 33

"My, my, my," Billy said with a snigger. "That little girl must've really been something."

"Beg your pardon?" Rob snapped around as he realized his brother was talking. They had been riding east out of Jacksonville, Texas for more than an hour, headed toward Palestine.

"I said, she must've really been something."

"Who?"

Billy doubled over in the saddle laughing.

"Well, what girl? Who are you talking about." Rob said defensively.

"Who do you think I'm talking about, idgit? The girl back at *Lola's Palace*. The one you spent two days locked in a bedroom with. What was her name, Alice?"

"Oh yeah, Alice," Rob said with a nod and grinned. "I was just thinking about her."

"Was she good?"

"Compared to what?"

Billy had to compose himself once more before answering.

"Yeah, I guess you wouldn't know. In other words, did you enjoy her company?"

"Yeah, I reckon I did. She was nice, and I liked her a lot." In his opinion, Alice was a nice girl who'd gotten turned around and headed the wrong way. They had spent the two days talking, playing checkers and reading, but there was no way he'd ever admit such things to his brother. In another place and a different time, he might have even liked her for more than a friend.

"Well, don't fall in love with her. You might not know it yet, but there's a lot of women just like Alice just waiting to meet you."

The brothers continued moving southeast for two weeks, not spending more than one or two nights at any given place. Each town they came to looked the same as the last one, Palestine, Buffalo and Franklin. None of them had a population over 180, and depended mostly on farming. What impressed Rob the most, was the devastation the drought was causing. Without rain, the crops in fields turned brown and brittle in the hot Texas sun and wind. They met several wagons headed east, as families, who had moved to Texas to start a new life, left their dreams and hopes lying in the burnt-out fields to be blown away with the topsoil.

Rob's thoughts turned toward the Russell family, and how lucky they were to have their fields located in bottom land that was irrigated by the Big Cypress Creek. He remembered how the earth had always felt cool and damp, compared to the parched, dry ground they were now crossing. Theodore and his family would never have to pack up and leave, unless the drought lasted long enough to dry up the Big Cypress, and Rob couldn't imagine that happening, although he reckoned it was possible.

Then, there was Clara Jean. He tried picturing her in his mind and could soon remember every little detail, down to the unruly hair poking from beneath her bonnet as they picked cotton. He could see her sunburned nose and freckles as she poked her pretty face between the plants and asked him questions. He could hear her laughing, and feel her lips against his as they kissed. He could even taste the tears on her cheeks when she knew he was leaving. Rob Mayfield suddenly felt dirty for having enjoyed his time with Alice. He closed his eyes and asked God to forgive him as his horse continued plodding across the sun-baked countryside. After all, he had seen her nude body, and it did cause lustful feelings to arise.

He reckoned the human mind to be a mighty powerful thing, because thoughts of Alice kept prodding their way into his reminiscing of Clara Jean. He struggled back and forth, knowing he had pledged his loved to Clara Jean, and had promised to return and marry her. But he had also enjoyed being with Alice. He had never known a woman could be so overpowering, and make a man feel that way. He could honestly see why Billy had turned out the way he had, but he also knew that enjoying such things was a sin, at least that's what he had been told. He renewed his vow to Clara Jean and prayed that God would help him stay true.

But what about married people? He couldn't imagine how they could sleep together and not enjoy doing the things that Alice had wanted him to do. After all, wasn't that how children were conceived? Rob began wondering what it would be like after he and Clara Jean got married. It didn't take much imagining for Clara's face to replace Alice inside the bedroom, and for the feel of Alice's skin to become Clara's as she pressed her nude breasts against his back. It suddenly felt right. He and Clara were man and wife, and it was okay. *Yeah*, he thought, as he rocked gently in the saddle. He and Clara Jean were married, and he had responsibilities. Right now, he had taken a trip with his brother to conduct some business. They would be away for several weeks, and while he was gone, his pretty wife would be home baking bread, and waiting for his return.

Rob Mayfield was thoroughly enjoying the world he had created when his brother's voice rudely interrupted his thoughts.

"Hey, wake up, little brother. We're almost there."

"Where?" Rob snapped his head upward.

"Rockdale. Where'd you think we were. Boy, that must've been some dream you were having."

"Why, did I say anything?"

"No, just grinning. Thinking about that girl back at Lola's?" Billy gave him a toothy grin.

"Something like that."

"Thought so. Well, once we get checked into a room and ourselves cleaned up, I'm sure we can find another Alice to keep you company."

Chapter 34

"Is this the place?" Al asked as they eyed the boarding house from across the street. The storekeeper at New Hope had kept his lips sealed tight, even while Gene and Albert were beating him. They left his lifeless body in a pool of blood and rode toward Tyler, thinking it might be the logical direction to find a gambler.

"That's what the bartender at the Trail Dust said."

"Think he got it right? Don't look much like a place a gambler would be hanging out to me," Gene said thoughtfully.

"Oh, he had it right," Vernon said with a snigger. "He remembered Bill Mayfield real well. Seems our friend beat the hell out of another gambler and killed one of his best customers. Then, him and his brother slipped outa Tyler in the middle of the night. He said the word was that Bill and the landlady had themselves a thing going."

"Really? Well now, that sounds more like the Bill Mayfield we know. What'd he say her name was," Gene asked.

"Wanda, Wanda Johnson. And from the way he described her, she's a right pretty woman."

"Well, maybe it's time for Wanda Johnson to meet the Lippert boys," Gene said, hitching his gunbelt.

Chapter 35

Rockdale was a far cry from the small farming communities they had just passed through, with a population of 1,700, five churches, two schools, and two steam powered gristmill and cotton gins. The town also had a 250-seat opera house, a bank and a newspaper office. The man who checked them into the hotel, said the town was given its name by a Mrs. B. F. Ackerman because of the huge rock that sat at the edge of town. It measured approximately twelve feet high and was twenty feet in diameter. Rob remembered seeing the boulder as they rode into town, but hadn't given it much attention. To him, it was simply a big rock with several boys playing on top.

Rockdale thrived because of the railroad. The International Great-Northern Railroad had sold off 400 acres that had been subdivided into lots in 1873, and the town sprang to life as a major shipping and supply point for the area farmers and ranchers. On the surface, the town looked prosperous. A train was loading and unloading passengers and a few goods as Rob and Billy walked the semi-busy street, looking for a place to eat. But being a farmer at heart, Rob was quick to notice the quiet mills, with their smokeless stacks poking toward a cloudless sky. The drought was having an effect on Rockdale as well.

The aroma of tortillas, chilies and cooking meat drew them toward a small Mexican cantina near the rail station. The sound of a guitar and a man singing in Spanish drifted through the opened window as Rob paused to glance once more at the quiet cotton gins.

"Come on, little brother," Billy said, pushing the door open. "My belly thinks I'm starving to death."

The thick adobe walls worked as an insulator against the heat, and the brothers stood in the cool dimness for a moment, allowing their eyes to adjust. An attractive girl with waist-length black hair excused herself from talking to two men at the bar and made her way toward them. The place was mostly empty, with only two tables being occupied. One was by an elderly Mexican couple eating dinner, and the other by two cowboys drinking beer and playing cards. A chubby, middle-aged man sat in the far corner with a bottle of tequila, playing the guitar and singing.

"*Buenos tardes, Señor*es. You may sit where you wish."

"Thank you kindly, Ma'am," Billy said, removing his hat.

"Down boy, take it easy." Rob sniggered as he followed his brother toward an empty table. "I know she's pretty, but let's eat first."

"Me? I thought I was gonna have to put a bridle on you, after *Lola's.*"

They chose a table next to the cowboys playing cards, and ordered two platefuls of tacos, rice and beans, with a pitcher of beer and two mugs. Rob made the mistake of copying one of the Mexicans seated at the bar, and dumped a healthy portion of the red sauce on his first taco without first tasting the concoction.

"Oh, God! Oh Jesus," he yelled, and almost downed an entire mug of beer, trying to kill the fire.

"I forgot you ain't used to this stuff. Better take it easy," Billy said, as Rob tried catching his breath. The *vaqueros* at the bar hooted along with the cowboys seated at the next table.

"There's shore a deck shy a joker," one of the men

said. He shuffled a deck of cards and continued talking as he dealt a hand.

"Best listen to yer pard, sonny, and go easy on that stuff. I made that mistake once myself. Now I just use it as a firing primer for my Henry rifle."

Billy watched the men play cards as they ate their dinner and he sipped his beer.

"Mind if I sit in on a hand or two," he asked after the girl had removed their plates and brought another pitcher of beer.

"If you're not looking to get rich. All we're doing is playing for pennies and killing time," the dealer said. As far as Rob knew, the one with a receding hairline, seated across from the dealer had not spoken a word since they entered the cantina.

"That's fine with me," Billy said and joined the men at their table. "Come on, Rob, and bring that pitcher with you. I'm Bill Mayfield," he added as Rob joined them, "and this is my kid brother, Rob."

"Pleased to meet you, gents," the dealer said. "I'm Kiowa Johnson, and that feller across the table happens to be Baldy Russell. He's got a burr under his saddle, so you'd best walk carefully 'round him."

"I'm right peaceable, to them that's peaceable to me." The man looked directly at Rob when he spoke, then continued eying Billy as the cards were shuffled.

"The anti is two cents," Kiowa said, and pitched two pennies toward the center of the table. He dealt a card to Billy and one to Baldy, then paused when he came to Rob.

"You in, boy? You ain't put no money on the table."

"No, I'm just watching."

"Huh, guess I won't be getting rich off this game," Kiowa said, and continued dealing.

"Won't get rich playing for pennies, anyway," Billy said, as he studied his hand. "Any place around town where a man can play for some real money?"

"More'n likely, but I don't know, 'cause we ain't looked," Kiowa said.

"Why not?"

"'Cause we like it here just fine," Baldy said.

"Look, mister, all I'm looking for is a friendly game and a little conversation. Okay? If you want me to leave, I will," Billy said, matching the man's stare.

"Whoa, you two." Kiowa waved a hand between the two men. "There's not enough money on the table to bury one, let alone both of you." He waited until the men turned their attention toward their cards and continued. "Good, now we can play cards and drink some beer."

They finished that hand, with the pot going to Kiowa, and the cards were passed to Billy, who shuffled and dealt them expertly. Everyone tossed in their two cent anti and began playing.

"Yes sir, this is much better. Besides, you two wouldn't want to tangle anyways," Kiowa said over his cards.

"Why's that," Baldy growled.

"Because this young pup's dying to make a name for hisself, and killing don't mean a thing to you."

"What's that supposed to mean?" Baldy laid his hand face down and glared.

"Nothing. Just that killing Billy here, wouldn't mean a thing to you, except they'd be adding one more to the list of things to hang you for. And Billy," Kiowa turned toward Billy with a grin, "he's probably shot a couple of men somewhere, but no one with worth mentioning. Why, he'd just love to go around bragging that he bored Baldy Russell, except I know he ain't fast enough, without seeing him draw. Now, ain't that right, son?"

"I don't know what you're driving at, but I don't like it," Billy said, scooting back from the table.

"Now, don't go getting your back up. I'm just making conversation, and trying to talk some sense into the both of you. Just calm down and let's go back to our game. No sense in spilling blood over a perfectly good deck of cards. First place, you come in here dressed in them fancy duds, wearing them pearl-handled pistols. Anyone dressed like that's wanting to attract attention. Which means he's looking to make a reputation for hisself, so he can't get upset when a feller like Baldy starts eyeing him suspicious-like.

"Thing is," he continued as they played, "he doesn't always know who he's bracing when someone gets their back up. Baldy and me's been pards over many a trail. But I happen to know he's no one to be trifled with, so I just get out of his way when things get stirred up. Believe me, boy," he stared intently at Billy, "you may look like King Fisher, but you ain't him, and you don't want to go bracing Baldy Russell. He's been an outlaw on the run longer'n you've been alive, and he's killed more men than you can count. You wouldn't stand a chance. Now, let's play some cards."

Kiowa tossed another penny into the pot and looked at Rob.

"Boy? Why don't you go fetch us another pitcher?"

"Yeah, sure."

Rob was waiting for the girl to refill the pitcher when Baldy Russell joined him at the bar.

"Don't mind my brother, Mr. Russell, he's just a little cocky."

"Mind him?" He smirked and began rolling a cigarette. "Na, I don't mind him. Not unless I have to kill him."

"That's what I was afraid of. My brother's kind of crazy at times. We had to leave several places because he got into trouble and shot some men."

"Did he kill any of them?" Baldy struck a match against the bar and lit his smoke.

"Yeah, two men. He just wounded the other."

"Were any of them gunfighters?"

"No, I don't think so. I knew Henry, the man he wounded, he was just a storekeeper. I think the one in Pittsburg was a farmer. He killed him. I don't really know about the other man...the one in Tyler, but I don't think he was a gunfighter."

"Huh," Baldy said with a slight grin, "didn't think so. I've seen wagonloads of boys like your brother, all looking to get a name for themselves. Ain't none of them I met lived long enough to get it done."

The girl slid the pitcher of beer on the counter and Baldy fished a dollar from his pocket.

"I heard you killed a man for killing your father," Rob said as Baldy grabbed the pitcher. "Is that true? I've got an uncle in Mitchell Bend who say's he knows your family, that's how I know," Rob added as Baldy returned the pitcher to the counter with a heavy sigh.

"Yeah, that's true. And I've been on the run ever since. And I've killed several men since, but only to stay alive. Killing's never fun, and it's no way to make a name for yourself, no matter what the cause."

"Yeah, but he deserved it if he killed your father. Didn't he?"

"Maybe so, but not the way I killed him. Look, the man lied in court and my daddy was hung for a crime he didn't commit, and they killed my little brother, when he tried busting the old man out of jail. So I got good and mad, and carried a grudge until it festered and boiled over. Then, instead of doing things the right way, I kicked his front door open and shot him in front of his wife. He might've deserved it, but she didn't. That was ten years ago, and there hasn't been a night since, that I haven't seen her with her husband's blood splattered across her face, screaming as she tried pushing his brains back into his skull. So, you keep that in mind, if you ever decide you need to kill someone.

"Take that brother of yours." He shifted his stare toward the two men playing cards. "He pictures himself to be some sort of shakes with cards and a gun, like King Fisher or Doc Holliday. But he hasn't faced a real gunfighter yet, and when he does, he's likely to get hisself killed."

"You mean, someone like you," Rob said.

"Or Kiowa. You see," Baldy paused as he retrieved the pitcher of beer and looked at Rob intently, "most men who are handy with a gun don't go around advertising. Kiowa might come across all friendly-like, but he's as quick as a rattler and twice as deadly when it comes to killing. Your brother, on the other hand, might be tolerable, but he's not quick enough, yet he struts around like a young peacock. He's looking to get hisself killed, and you following after him will only mean the both of you dying. Take my advice, and go back where you came from. Leave your brother to his own devices."

Rob watched as the big man returned to the table, carrying the pitcher of beer. He had just carried on a conversation with the notorious outlaw Baldy Russell, and the man's words left him stunned.

******

It was getting late, and Rob's stomach was growling. He ordered more tacos and beer for everyone, and sat watching as the three men continued their penny-anti card game. His tongue felt numb from the amount of beer he had consumed, so he continued heaping the red sauce onto his tacos.

"Oooee, Pard," Kiowa said as Rob bit into one. "You might not be able to feel that liquid fire right now, but you're shore gonna feel it tomorrow in the outhouse."

"Better take a bucket of water with you, that's for

sure," Baldy said with a snigger.

"You mentioned King Fisher earlier," Billy said as he shuffled the deck.

"We did?" Kiowa eyed Billy over his mug of beer.

"Yeah, you did. You said I looked something like him."

"Well now, I was referring to the duds you're sporting. The spurs and pearl-handled pistols and whatnot. It's been more'n a year since I tipped a glass with King, but I recollect he used to be a bit taller'n you and had on them fancy chaps he always wore."

"What do you mean, *used to be* taller than me? He didn't shrink, did he," Billy said with a laugh as he dealt the cards.

"No, don't reckon he shrank. He might still be taller...all stretched out like he is." Kiowa picked up the cards and fanned his hand.

"*Stretched out*? What's he talking about?" Billy looked toward Baldy, who just snickered and continued looking at his cards.

"Guess you ain't heard the news. King went and got hisself killed," Kiowa said matter-of-factly. "Him and ol' Ben Thompson both. Deader'n Moses."

"Dead? What happened?"

Rob stared with a taco halfway to his mouth as Billy received the news of his hero's death. There was genuine concern in his voice.

"Well sir, as I heard it, they walked into *Vaudeville Variety Theater* in San Antonio pretty as you please, sometime last March. That was kind of a fool thing for them to do, seeing as Thompson had killed one of its owners over a gambling debt. Anyway, they were both drunker'n skunks, when Ben starts causing a ruckus, saying he wants to see Joe Foster and shake hands or have a drink. Well, Joe's the partner of the man he killed, so Foster says okie-dokie, and has them moved to the upstairs balcony. But, instead of getting the truce he wanted, they both got filled with lead. They claim Ben Thompson was hit three or four times in the head, and several more times in the body. King got something like thirteen holes bored into him, including a couple in the noggin." He paused and gave Billy a cold stare.

"Thing is, neither Ben Thompson or John King Fisher had time to draw. They both were some shakes with an iron, but they died with their guns holstered.

Chapter 36

"How much money do you have on you?"

"I don't know," Rob said, fishing inside his pockets. "Oh, about five dollars is all. I just paid our bill at the livery. Why? How much you got?" They had just finished buying rolling tobacco, shaving soap and boot polish, and were now standing in front of the general store talking while Billy rolled a cigarette.

"Twenty. I had a run of bad luck at the table. An old toothless man almost picked my pockets dry before I knew what was happening," Billy said with a laugh.

"Do you think he was cheating?"

"No, that's what's funny about it. The old coot was just better'n me." Billy licked the paper and propped the cigarette in the corner of his mouth to light.

"I would have liked sitting there awhile longer, to figure out what he was doing, but thought I'd better quit while I still had a few dollars in my pocket."

"What are we going to do now? Want me to see if they need help at the livery?" Rob asked the question as he studied the money in his hand.

"Work in the livery? Hush your mouth, little brother." Billy grinned and lit the cigarette. "No, I figured we'd move on while we've still got a small stake, and find ourselves a new game. Austin's only thirty or forty miles down the road, and I had me some luck last time I was there. Why don't you get the horses and..." Billy trailed off as an angry fat man exited the store, yelling at a middle-aged woman.

"I'm tired of hearing excuses, Mrs. Green. Michael has been extending your credit behind my back long enough. I felt sorry for you after your husband died, and was generous enough to give you credit. But you owe too much as it is, and feeding four children, there's no way you'll ever pay your bill, so no more. Do you understand me? No more! If you can't pay your bill, then you'll just have to find another store to do your shopping in." He turned and began yelling at the grocery clerk who was standing in the doorway, while a well dressed woman brushed passed the clerk and climbed into a carriage as if nothing of this was happening.

"I own this store, Michael Jenkins, and I warned you several months ago to quit extending credit to those who can't pay their bills."

"Yes, but they need to eat..." the clerk started.

"Enough! Do you understand me? Enough! I'll deal with you later." He climbed into the carriage next to the woman and shook the reins.

"My, my, my," Billy said, as the carriage moved away. "Here, give me your money."

Rob passed his last five dollars to his brother and watched as Billy fished his twenty dollar gold piece from his pocket, and pressed the money into the woman's hands.

"Here, ma'am. It ain't much, but it's all we've got. Now, you take this and buy something to feed your young'ns with."

"Oh, my, I, I, I can't take your money," she stammered as a tear rolled down one cheek. A crowd had now gathered. Some were casting angry glances and dispersions toward the retreating buggy, while others murmured words of sympathy toward the widow.

"Sure you can, 'cause we're giving it as a gift, and we won't be taking it back. Ain't that right little brother?"

"Yeah, sure," Rob said.

"I don't know who you are, Mister," the storekeeper said, slipping an arm around the now weeping lady, "but that's the kindest thing I've seen anyone do today. Especially after listening to Basil Semmens."

"He's the fellow that just left," Billy asked.

"Yes, the greedy bastard! Sorry, Mrs. Green."

The woman smiled, then fished a handkerchief from her handbag and blew her nose. A large man with a star on his vest pushed his way through the crowd.

"What's going on?"

"Oh, just Basil and his wife hollerin' and trying to starve the poor out of existence," a tall lanky man said with a snigger.

"That right?" The sheriff hitched his britches and stared as the buggy disappeared behind one of the cotton gins in a cloud of dust.

"Yes," the storekeeper snorted, "the old skinflint withdrew a hunk of money from the bank, then went around collecting rent from nearly everyone in town, including me. He claims he's nearly broke, but he's carrying a wad that'd choke a horse."

"What's he doing carrying that much cash?" The crease in the sheriff's brow grew deeper.

"His wife bragged that they're about to take a trip to Austin to do some shopping. He makes his money off us, then spends it somewhere else. Anyway, he just got through saying folks who's got needs, like Mrs. Green, aren't welcome inside his store. He got downright rude and embarrassing. Then these two young men dug into their pockets to help her out," the storekeeper said.

"That was mighty kind of you." The sheriff eyed Billy up and down, then allowed his gaze to rest on the pistols. "Wish more folks would do that sort of thing."

"I, I really do thank you, but I can't take your

money," Mrs. Green said, and tried returning the money to Billy once again.

"That ain't our money," he said holding his hands in the air and shaking his head. "It's your money now. The good Lord told us to give it to you, and that's exactly what we did. You aren't for going against Almighty God, are you?"

"No, since you put it that way. I, I don't know what to say…"

"Then, don't say anything, Ma'am. Rob and me lost our ma a few months back, and we count it a pleasure giving folks a helping hand whenever we can." Billy squeezed the woman's hand, and kissed her on the cheek.

"Wait, I don't know your names," she said and Billy moved away.

"Mayfield, Ma'am. Bill and Rob Mayfield. We're Lucile's boys from Douglass."

"Well, God bless you…both of you," the woman said as Billy turned away.

"Just a minute, you two." The voice came from the sheriff, and Billy halted with a sigh, but turned to give the lawman a grin.

"Yes, what is it Sheriff?"

"I've been keeping an eye on you two, especially you, toting those fancy guns, and I haven't quite got you figured out."

"There isn't much to figure, Sheriff. We're just a couple of Texicans, working our way south. We thought we'd spend a couple of days here, resting…maybe find a friendly card game or two. But," Billy sniggered, "that old man across the street nearly picked my pockets clean. That little bit I gave that woman was the last money we had, so I reckon we'll just mosey on down to Austin and see if we can't rustle up a grub steak."

"Huh," the lawman said with a grin. "Yeah, you're

not the first one that's had his pockets picked by Howard. He's more'n likely the best hand with a deck of cards in Texas. I guess I kind of had you figured wrong. I was expecting you to be trouble, but you've kept your nose pretty clean. Keep it that way, and you're welcome in Rockdale anytime."

"Thank you, Sheriff, but we'll be moseying now. We might stop back by sometime, on our way home."

"What'll we do now, Billy," Rob asked as they walked toward the livery.

"We're going to Austin, just like I told the sheriff."

"I mean, what are we going to live on? We're broke."

"Oh, I've got a plan. Just don't you worry, little brother. We'll be rolling in money before nightfall."

Chapter 37

"Why are we headed this way, Billy? Austin's east of here," Rob said as Billy turned south, past the grist and cotton gins.

"Sure is, unless they've moved it."

"Come on, Billy. Why are we heading south?" Rob had to spur his horse to keep up with Billy's bay.

"Because this is the way that fat bastard went. I want to have a little talk with him."

"Why?"

"Jesus, little brother! Quit asking so many questions. I'll explain later," Billy said, and urged his horse into a full gallop.

The horses were eager to run, after being cooped inside the livery for several days, and they allowed them to have their head, then reined them back as the buggy came into view. The driver had set the speed of the buggy at a quick trot, and it was easy for the fresh horses to overtake the rig. Billy pulled his horse to the side the driver was on as they drew near, and motioned for Rob to pass on the opposite. Billy smiled and tipped his hat as he galloped past, then grabbed the horse's bridle, bringing the buggy to a halt.

"Here now! What's the meaning of this," the fat man bellowed.

"Why I never...! You let go of our horse this instant," his wife hissed.

"Yes, Ma'am, this instant." Billy smiled and tipped his hat toward the woman. "Mr. Basil Semmens, sir?"

149

"Yes. I remember seeing you in town, in front of the store. Is there anything wrong?"

"Why there sure is. There's a whole lot of things wrong. Like the way you was hollerin' and treating that poor widow-woman in front of all those people."

"Edith Green owes the store more money than she'll ever be able to repay, and I own the store, so how I treat her is none of your concern."

"Oh, but it is."

Rob stifled a cry when his brother pointed a pistol at Basil Semmens and cocked the hammer.

"Now take that belly-gun out with two fingers and toss it on the ground. Come on," he said as Semmens gave him a blank stare, "I'll shoot you, if you make me get it myself. Easy, just two fingers," he added as the man reached to the gun hidden under his coat.

"You…you can't do this! This is robbery," Semmens bellowed as he tossed the small pistol into the dirt.

"You should know all about that. Stealing food out of widow's mouths, and overcharging folks for groceries and rent. Yes, sir, you catch on fast. Now, you lady," Billy gestured with his gun, "reach behind the seat real careful, and toss that shotgun. Come on, woman. I saw it when I passed the buggy. I'll shoot the both of you if I have to come over there and get it myself."

"I never…I'll tell the sheriff about this," she growled and snorted as she tossed the doubled barreled weapon in the dust.

"Yes, Ma'am, I reckon you will…whenever you get back to town. Little brother, start unhitching their horse."

"What?"

"Unhitch their horse. Go on," he said as Rob hesitated.

"You, you can't take our horse and leave us stranded out here." Semmens paled as Rob unhitched the white mare from the buggy.

"Oh, you'll get it back, we're not horse thieves. Besides, they hang folks for that sort of thing in Texas. But I reckon I could shoot the both of you, and no one would give much of a damn. Now, empty your pockets. Come on mister," he added as Semmens stared. "I'm starting to lose patience. Toss me your jacket and turn your pants pockets inside out. And you, lady, give my little brother your handbag."

"I will not!"

"Okay," Billy said, and sent a bullet that clipped the brim of her bonnet. The woman threw the handbag at Rob, as Basil removed his jacket and emptied the contents from inside his pants pockets.

"There, now see how easy everything is, when we come to an understanding?"

"What do you want me to do with the handbag?" Rob held the bag with trembling hands.

"Just take the money and give it back," Billy said as he emptied the man's billfold. "Whoa, you *could* choke a horse with this, just like they said back in town." He waved the wad of bills in the air.

"You can't leave us like this," Semmens gasped, "with no horse or money. That's our life savings. We don't even have any water."

"Well, now, look who's suddenly needy and begging for mercy, little brother," Billy said with a snigger. "Like I said, you'll get your horse back, and I doubt if this is all the money you've got stuck inside that bank. Besides, it wouldn't take you long to get it back, the way you suck blood out of the folks in Rockdale. And anyone who would travel anywhere in Texas without water deserves to die of thirst."

He stuffed the money in his pocket and tossed the man his coat, then calmly holstered his gun.

"You know, little brother, I think these folks might have a different outlook on life now." He talked as he unloaded Semmens' shotgun and pistol and gave them both a toss. "Of course, being as mean and nasty as they both are, I doubt they'll treat folks any different. I bet they'll hire someone to ride shotgun when they go on their little trips and carry money." He climbed back onto his horse and tipped his hat.

"I probably won't be seeing you again, unless I hear you've been mistreating that poor widow back in town. Then, I'll pay you another visit, but if not, y'all have a good day. Come on, little brother, bring that nag of theirs, and let's ride."

Billy urged his horse into a gentle lope toward Rockdale, and waited until they had almost reached the edge of town, before sending Semmens' horse back down the road with a good swat on the butt. Rob was stunned when his brother insisted on riding through the middle of town as bold as brass, where he stopped at the store and paid Edith Green's outstanding grocery bill with the stolen money. He bought a few more supplies and told the storekeeper he had had a run of luck at a card table, then left town at a leisurely pace. They were well down the road toward Austin before Rob broke his self-imposed silence.

"Good Lord, Billy. You know what you just did? You robbed that poor man, and made me a thief in the process!"

"*Poor man*? Where the hell have you been, little brother? That fat man's the biggest thief around. I simply took a little of his stolen money and paid that widow's food bill, which…if he was such a fine Christian…he would've done in the first place. He should've taken care of her and those children without asking a dime."

"Yeah, I agree with that part. But they know who we are, and they're gonna lock us up when they catch us."

"No, wrong again, little brother. You need to know which battles to pick. I let them know who we are for a reason. That old skinflint bastard's so mean, everyone in Rockdale, including the sheriff, hates his guts. He'll bust his rear getting back to Rockdale, then pitch a royal fit, demanding the sheriff gets a posse and goes after us. But, the town's people will remember we're the kindhearted brothers that gave their last few dollars to help a widow, when they know what an ass he is. I doubt the sheriff could get much of a posse together if he wanted to, and I also doubt that they'd travel more'n three or four miles either direction looking for us. Oh, the sheriff might send a telegram or two to Austin, asking them to keep an eye out for us, but I'm not sure he'll even do that. And if they did happen to catch us, what do you think a jury of town's people in Rockdale would convict us of? Being nice to a widow? Pick your battles little brother."

"You didn't seem to think that way when you shot that man in Tyler," Rob said sullenly.

"That man was a card cheat who tried to kill me behind the saloon. Besides, I *did* add insurance by stopping at *Lola's Palace*."

"*Lola's?*"

"Yeah," Billy glanced at him with a grin. "Remember? I gave Lola more than twice what she was asking for our room and board. If anyone came looking for us, she'd tell them we'd never been there, or send them in the opposite direction. And," he pointed at Rob, "you can bet your last penny, little brother, either one of us will be welcome at her palace anytime we choose. Might be kind of fun to visit Alice again when we're finished in Cool Water. What do think?"

Rob didn't answer. Billy had given him too much to think about. Most of what he said seemed right. Basil Semmens was a greedy thief, stealing from folks in Rockdale and mistreating widows. But Rob couldn't see how he and

Billy becoming thieves by stealing from another thief was going to help matters. As far as Alice and her wonderland was concerned, that drug up another wagonload of things for him to deal with.

Chapter 38

"Yeah, I sort of remember seeing a feller who looked something like that. What're ya looking for him fer?" The man looked to be in his fifties, and leaned heavily against the bar rubbing the gray stubble on his chin.

"We've got a message for him. Our brother Harry died," Vernon said with a growl.

"Oh? Is he some sort of kin of y'all?"

"Yeah. You might say we're sort of cousins…distant cousins," Gene Lippert said. "Him and Harry were pretty close."

"Mmmm, too bad." He swirled the last inch of his lukewarm beer, gulping it in one swallow.

"What's too bad," Vernon asked.

"About losing your brother…the one that died."

"Yeah," Vernon agreed with a nod. "It sort of took us by surprise."

"We're wasting time," Albert barked, and slammed his empty mug against the bar.

"Take it easy, Al," Vernon said with a snicker. "We've waited this long, a few more minutes won't hurt. Barkeep," he raised his voice and motioned toward their mugs. "Another round for us and our new friend.

"Now," he said with a grin, "where'd you say cousin Billy's been keeping hisself?"

"I seen him the other day at Lola's Palace. It's a fancy whorehouse just outside of town. Of course, you didn't hear me say none of this, understand, 'cause my wife wouldn't cotton to my being at such a place."

"No, most wives wouldn't," Vernon said with a laugh as he slapped the man on the back. "Your secret is safe with us. Now tell me, where do we find this Lola's Palace?"

"Take the road north toward Tyler, and you'll see it sitting amongst some trees about a half a mile out of town. Right pretty place. Used to belong to a feller who had some money back before the war. He got hisself killed at Gettysburg, and the family sold the house to Lola. I hear she's got some real pretty girls and does a brisk business. Of course I wouldn't know personally, understand."

"No, of course not." Vernon laughed.

They were close, and he could feel the excitement building inside his bones. He had known they were close the moment they discovered the boarding house the Mayfield brothers had stayed in back in Tyler. The landlady had put up an argument of sorts, but caved after Vernon had hit her only five or six times. They left her lying on the bedroom floor with a tear-streaked face and a broken nose.

"Drink up boys," Vernon hoisted his mug high in the air, "it's about time to go see cousin Billy."

Chapter 39

Rob had never been to Austin, and was awed by its teeming population of more than eleven thousand. Having been established as the Texas state capital during the statewide election of 1872, many of the residents had expected Austin to become an economic power, but it instead had emerged as an educational center. The city boasted of its own public school system and three colleges, counting the University of Texas.

After checking into a hotel, Billy walked the streets boldly, dressed in his black hat, shiny boots and proudly displaying the pearl-handled guns. Rob, on the other hand, locked himself inside their hotel room after supper, certain the law would soon knock on the door and arrest him for robbery. He was relieved when Billy, after spending only two days, decided it was time to leave Austin and head south to San Antonio.

Chapter 40

Rob was stunned at San Antonio, and followed his brother in a daze as they wove their way through the busy streets. While Austin had been an educational hub, San Antonio was the economic hub of southern Texas. The city was the center of cattle trail drives, as well as distribution, mercantile and military center serving the border region. It boasted of two railroads, with more being built, and had developed an important wool market to serve the merino sheepherders in the adjacent hill country.

Founded in 1718 by the Spanish as the site of *San Antonio de Valero Mission*, San Antonio quickly earned its reputation as a friendly, but tough town. The mission was turned into a military barracks in 1795, and the name was changed to *Alamo*. During the Texas Revolution, San Antonio was the site of several battles, including the siege of Bexar and the battle of the Alamo. A failed attempt to negotiate with the Comanche Indians resulted in an open battle in the streets in 1840, and the town was seized twice during the Mexican invasions of 1842, making it one of the most fought-over cities in North America. Texas joined the South during the Civil War, and the local militia forced the surrender of the federal arsenal located at San Antonio, before the state seceded on March 2, 1877. After Texas seceded from the Union, San Antonio served as a Confederate depot, and several units, such as John S. Ford's Cavalry of the West were stationed there, but the city was somehow removed from the fighting.

The population had mushroomed to more than twenty thousand by the time the Mayfield brothers arrived, and was growing daily. The citizens were mainly a mix of Mexican, German, Southern Anglo and a few former black slaves, who built their housing and places of business to their own liking. Old Spanish walls remained beside modern structures and Victorian mansions.

"Better close that mouth, before you swallow a fly," Billy said with a snigger as they dismounted at one of the several livery stables. "Quite a city, isn't it?"

"I never dreamed anything like this existed. I mean, I've read about large cities, but didn't think something like this was in Texas."

"Oh, you haven't seen anything yet, little brother. We're not really even into town. I'll show you some real sights before we're through."

Billy insisted on checking them into one of the finest hotels. After hot baths and a change of clean clothes, they ate at one of the best restaurants, then took in a show which included crude jokes by distastefully dressed men and scantily-clad dancing girls. It was approaching eleven o'clock when Rob returned to their room and collapsed on the bed in exhaustion. He was thinking of the girls dancing across the stage, lifting their dresses and kicking their long stockinged legs high in the air when he fell asleep. He was dreaming of Clara Jean when Billy entered the room sometime around one in the morning. Billy smelled of liquor and stale tobacco, but that wasn't what irritated Rob. He had been inside Clara Jean's bedroom, watching her dance around the room, dressed in nothing but her unmentionables, kicking her long legs high in the air. She was dancing for him alone, and the sight excited Rob. Billy's entering the room had caused her to vanish. He rolled over and covered his head with the feather pillow as Billy removed one boot, then the other, allowing them to clunk noisily against the floor. Rob squeezed his eyes shut, trying to will Clara Jean to continue her dance, but she was gone.

Chapter 41

Billy was seated at the table studying the cards in his hand. He had spent the past two days winning small amounts at different tables, but had been on a steady losing streak for the past two hours. He grinned at the man seated across the table, dressed in similar attire to his own. He knew the man's name was Howard, and also knew he had been cheating, but hadn't quite figured out how, until the man seated to his left ordered another drink. Most dealers, even the good ones, win approximately sixty to seventy percent of the time, especially if they want a busy table. But in Billy's estimation, this man had been winning eighty to ninety percent of the hands dealt, maybe higher. But Billy had finally discovered the man's secret, and his luck was about to change.

"Say, darlin'," he said as the waitress passed, "what'd you say your name was?"

"Why, it's Sugar, and shame on you for forgettin' so soon." She would have been attractive without the heavy layers of eye makeup and lip rouge. She gave him an ample view of her cleavage as she bent to caress his cheek with a soft hand. Bill returned her smile and dropped a twenty-dollar gold piece down the front of her dress.

"Why, thank you, honey. What's that for?"

"That's for being a good girl, and taking such good care of this table."

"You're quite welcome, but I was only doing my little-ole job." She flashed him a set of white teeth.

"That's what I figured. You've only served two other

tables tonight, but spent most of your time hovering around this one," Billy said, taking another peek at his cards.

"That's what she gets paid for. I tip her extra to keep people at my table supplied with something to drink and a little female companionship. Now, let's get back to our game," the dealer said with a growl.

"Oh, I bet you do tip her well," Billy said with a laugh.

"And, what's that supposed to mean?" The dealer slapped his cards down on the table and glared.

"Exactly what it's supposed to mean." Billy glanced at the other four men seated at the table.

"Didn't any of you think it odd that Sugar's been taking extra good care of you?"

"Well, no. I kind of like her hanging around and filling my glass when it gets empty," said the man seated to the right of the dealer.

"Satisfied? Now, let's get back to our game, that is, unless you have something else to say," the dealer said.

"Yes, as a matter of fact I do."

"Hey," Sugar said as Billy jerked the empty tray from her hands.

"See the bottom of this tray, boys?" He held toward the other gamblers.

"Yeah, so," one of them said.

"It looks like a mirror. She's been showing our friend at the head of the table what you're holding, every time she fills you glass, or pats your cheek." He casually rocked the tray as he spoke, and the cards held by the man seated on his right suddenly appeared in the shiny metal surface. "I happened to glance up as she served Doug a minute ago, and can tell you Doug is holding two deuces, a seven of hearts, an eight of clubs and a nine of hearts. Our dealer knows that also, because I caught him looking at the tray."

"No, he's lying," Sugar said, backing away from the

162

table. "I don't know how you could say such a thing. I never did any of that. Honest!"

"Mister, I believe you just called me a cheat." The dealer rose from his seat as people vacated their tables.

"I figure it fits. Now, just so you know before you do something foolish, I killed a man a couple of weeks ago for doing the same thing. So, sit down before you make another mistake."

"I don't think he's bluffing, Howard," the dealer at the next table said with a laugh. He was the only one who had not vacated his seat, and sat calmly shuffling his deck. "I warned you about doing that several times. It's pretty obvious, especially to someone who's been around a little. From the looks of him, our friend might be on the young side, but I've got a feeling he's seasoned with alkali. Actually, I'm surprised you and Sugar's survived this long. I would have killed you both if I caught you cheating."

"I thought about it," Billy said, revealing the cocked pistol in his left hand. The dealer paled at the sight of the gun. "Now, are we going to sit like gentlemen, and finish our game? Or, am I going to have to kill you? The choice is yours. Make your call, Howard."

Howard took his seat and downed a shot of whiskey in one gulp.

"There, now isn't that better than me splattering your brains all over the room? Oh, I almost forgot," Billy turned toward the frightened waitress, "here's you tray, Sugar. Why don't you forget about our table for an hour or so? I'm sure one of us can fetch our own drinks."

"Yes, sir," she said, and scampered away.

"Now, what do you say, gentlemen? A new game?"

Billy grinned at the men as they took their seats.

"Yeah, and you deal," one of the men growled as he snatched the deck from Howard's hand.

"Na-uh," a second man said and grabbed the dealer's

sleeve as he started from the table. "Yer gonna sit there and take yer medicine. You've been fleecing us all night, now it's our turn."

"Five card draw sound okay?" Billy smiled as he dealt the cards. His luck was holding, and getting better by the day. Nothing could stop him now, and who could tell where it would end? He might even be bigger than King Fisher, especially since the king had been stupid enough to get himself killed.

Although never actually meeting the man, Billy had always admired John King Fisher, and wanted to emulate him. Fisher was fast with a gun and had built an empire by the time he was thirty, with him as supreme monarch. No one argued or questioned his decisions. He dressed as he wished, tossed money around, and handed power to whomever he wanted, and revoked it the same way. King Fisher owned a large ranch on Pendencia Creek near Eagle Pass and had a sign posted on the main road saying, *This is King Fisher's road, take the other one.* King Fisher ruled as he wished, and his beautiful queen, Sarah Vivian had given him four lovely daughters, but no sons. Billy wondered how large his own kingdom would be when he reached thirty. He believed it would be much larger, because he was smarter and had learned from Fisher's mistakes.

In Bill's estimation, John King Fisher had been stupid concerning his friendship with Ben Thompson. He had checked, while in Austin, and everything Kiowa Johnson said was true. Thompson might have been fast and deadly in his day, and had even served as City Marshall for Austin for a period of time, but he was also a drunk, and alcohol had taken its effect. At the time of his death, Ben Thompson was way past his prime as a gunfighter, and King Fisher had been stupid to associate with him.

Billy Mayfield vowed he would never make that mistake. He never allowed himself to become intoxicated, especially while gambling, because the hours spent at the card table were working hours. He also never allowed himself any close ties to anyone. His relationships with Wanda Johnson and Rob had been the exception, and if need be, both were expendable. He had hoped to make Rob a part of his kingdom, ruling as some sort of vice president, but Rob was dying to return to the cotton fields and that skinny girl in Pittsburg. He decided the best thing he could do was, after they had finished in Cool Water, cut Rob loose and send him on his way. Wanda, on the other hand, had been something else. He might send for her, once he had established his kingdom. That is, if he hadn't met someone better by then.

He smiled as he dealt the cards with precision, allowing each man, excluding the former dealer, Howard, to win at least one hand. He waited until he had gained their confidence, then began gradually taking a pot here and there, until he was winning about sixty percent of the time, but still keeping the players happy. When Billy left the saloon around one o'clock in the morning, his pockets were again filled with winnings, and he had decided it was time to move on. It was almost time to visit Cool Water.

Chapter 42

Lola was a much harder nut to crack than Wanda Johnson, and it excited Vernon. He liked it when a woman put up a good fight, and it didn't matter whether the fight was in the bedroom or on a busy street, the result was the same. They had been arguing several minutes, and the tingling sensation grew the longer she resisted. He doubled his fist and hit her again, knocking her to the floor, but instead of caving like Wanda, the attractive woman set her lips into a thin line and yelled.

"I told you I don't give out my client's personal information, so get the hell out." Vernon didn't believe Lola to be her real name, any more than the names used by the rest of the whores.

"No? You're gonna tell me whether it's your policy or not. Now, I'm only gonna ask nicely one more time. Where's Bill Mayfield?"

A skinny blond stuck her head through the doorway and shouted, "Don't tell them, Lola. These are the guys Rob was telling me about!"

"I know who they are, Alice. Now, get out of here...all of you!"

"No. You, Alice or whatever your name is, come here." Vernon motioned toward the girl.

"I said get out of here. George!" Lola screamed the name and a man charged through the rear door carrying a shot gun. He was greeted by several bullets fired from Albert and Gene's pistols.

"What the hell?" One of the clients charged downstairs in his long-johns, carrying a gun. He, along with several others who made the mistake of leaving their rooms, were cut-down in a hail of gunfire.

"Now that we've established some rules," Vernon said, grabbing Alice by the hair and dragging her to face Lola, "I'll ask once again. Where's Bill Mayfield?"

"You bastard!"

"Still not ready to talk?" He twisted Alice's arm behind her back, and the girl screamed as the bone snapped.

"Damn, girl, better get some meat on your bones." Vernon sniggered as Alice crumbled in a sobbing heap. "That was too easy." He grabbed her by the hair and jerked her upward.

"Gonna tell me now, or do I break her other arm?"

"Leave her alone!" Lola leaped at him with her long fingernails and got knocked to the floor for the effort. He promptly broke Alice's left arm and motioned toward his brothers.

"Bring me another girl." He stared Lola in the eye as screams and the sound of scuffles could be heard in the next room. "You're gonna tell me where he went, woman, even if I bust every bone in every whore you've got working here."

"Let me kill this one, Vern," Gene said as he drug a hysterical chunky brunette into the room.

"Na, I'll handle it. You beat that storekeeper clean to death without getting him to talk."

"Oh, God, please no! Don't hurt me," the girl sobbed and begged.

"Get over here!" He yanked her hair, shaking her head back and forth.

"You'll have to excuse Gene some," he said to Lola. "He ain't quiet been right since a Yankee bounced a mini-ball off his head. So, what's it gonna be? You gonna talk, or am I gonna have to bust her up?" He gave her arm a twist, causing her to scream.

"No, no! Don't hurt any more of my girls," Lola said from where she was kneeling beside Alice. "I'll tell you what I know."

"Well now, that's being a little more sensible. None of this would've happened if you would've told us in the first place. "Where's Bill Mayfield?"

"I don't know exactly, but he mentioned to one of the girls he was going to Cool Water. He said someone owed him a lot of money."

"Cool Water? Where the hell's that?"

"I don't know. Somewhere near the border. I heard him mention Carrizo Springs once. Maybe it's near there."

"What else can you tell me?"

"Nothing...I swear! Now, will you please leave us alone? I'd like to help these people if I can."

"Sure," Vernon said with a snigger. "But you'd best hope you're not lying. 'Cause if you are, I'll be coming back to finish what we started."

"That's all I know...honest. Now please go!"

"Yeah, we're going. Come on, boys, let's find our friend Billy."

They left out the front in entrance, but not before Gene laid the chunky brunette's scalp open with the butt of his pistol.

Chapter 43

Carrizo Springs sat in the middle of Dimmit County, bordering Maverick and Zalvalda Counties, near the Mexican border, surrounded by grassland, filled with brush and cactus. Under normal conditions, the Nueces and the Frio Rivers flowed freely, helping spring-fed streams and lakes keep large herds of cattle, sheep, horses and farmers supplied with ample water. But the lack of rain was beginning to take its toll here also, as many of the smaller streams they crossed were either dry or down to a trickle, while lakes and ponds were showing large amounts of brown earth that had once been covered with water. The cattle and horses that had once roamed free, were grazing closer toward the rivers.

The earliest Americans to settle at Carrizo Springs were hearty men, like James Roberts, William McLauglin, Silas Hay, Constant Terry, and ex-slave Bob Lemmons. They, along with others, banded together mainly for protection against the constant Indian attacks, but they also found the land was cheap and the springs offered a bountiful supply of water. It was hard times for the settlers. They were still experiencing occasional Indian attacks when the Mayfield brothers arrived, as well as raids from Mexican bandits and American outlaws. While Captain Levi English had organized the settlers into a militia to defend themselves, Dimmit County still earned its reputation of being a *no man's land*.

There were a few modern dwellings scattered along

the streets, and a court house was currently under construction, but a large portion of the houses were *jacales*, copies of the Mexican huts surrounding the area. The walls of the *jacales* were constructed of pickets of mesquite or elm taken from the creeks, and lashed together with smaller branches and rawhide, then plastered on the inside with a mixture of clay and gravel. Carrizo Springs was only thirty miles or so south of San Antonio, but Rob felt as though he had arrived in a different world.

Billy stopped at a crude stable at the far end of town and dismounted. Rob lingered in the saddle awhile longer, taking in the thatched stable and corral made of crooked mesquite branches, while Billy addressed the owner in Spanish.

"Come on, little brother, Miguel will stable our horses," Billy said, tossing the owner a gold coin.

"Think it's safe to leave them here?"

"Safer than San Antonio," Billy said, untying his saddlebags. "Miguel was a pistolero, and rode and fought with some of the best, until he took a bullet in the hip." He tossed the bags across one shoulder and waited as Rob fumbled with the thongs holding his saddlebags. "Miguel may not ride too well, but it hasn't slowed his gun hand, and the last man who tried stealing a horse from this stable paid with his life."

******

They bought drinks at a small cantina not too far from Miguel's stables, where Billy became involved in a card game. Rob soon lost interest in watching his brother's skill with cards, and was beginning to feel the effects of three beers on an empty stomach. He decided against eating inside the cantina, after watching flies crawl across a hunk of raw meat and a pan of stale refried beans, and excused himself. He steadied himself against the side of the building when the bright sunlight hit him, then wandered down the street looking for a cleaner place to eat. He hadn't gone far when the smell of spicy meat and fresh-cooked tortillas assailed his nostrils, causing his stomach to growl loudly. The aroma was coming from a *jacale*, where an attractive Mexican woman was bent over an open-air adobe stove in the yard. He watched as she tossed several corn tortillas on a metal grate and cringed as she turned them with her bare fingers, wondering how she kept from burning herself on the flames licking the bottom of the grate.

"*Me excusa*," Rob said in halting Spanish. "*Usted sabe de un luger que puedo comprar algo comer?*"

The woman glanced up at him, and flashed a smile before turning back toward the tortillas. He only caught a glimpse of her face, but it was enough to know she was beautiful.

"*Si*," she said, removing the tortillas with deft fingers. "*Usted puede comer aqua, si usted desea.*"

Lordy, he thought as his stomach gave another growl. *I hope I understood her right. I think she just said I can eat here.*

"*Gracias*, but I don't speak good Spanish."

"That's okay, *Señor*. I speak English," she said, holding the basket of hot tortillas. "My name is Teresa. Come," she motioned with her head as she turned toward the *jacale*, "you may come into my *casa*."

The inside of the hut was clean and surprisingly cool, with a breeze blowing through the opened windows. An elderly white-haired woman was lying on a cot in one corner, and a sleeping dog in the middle of the floor opened his eyes to acknowledge Rob's presence, then closed them again.

"Is that your mother," Rob asked, as she propped the woman up, and began feeding her soup.

"*No, e'ste es mi abuela.*"

"I beg your pardon, Ma'am?"

"Yolanda is my grandmother. She is like my mother, because she raised me since I was a little child." She continued spooning the liquid into the old woman's mouth as she talked. "My mama and papa both died when I was very young."

"I'm sorry."

"*Gracias.* But *mi abuela* took me and loved me when I needed her most." She wiped the woman's mouth and kissed her forehead. From the blank stare in the old woman's eyes, Rob doubted if she was aware of her surroundings. "This *casa* was hers. My grandfather built it with his own hands. Now that she is old and sick, I shall love and care for her." She placed the bowl on the table and motioned toward a chair.

"*Sie'ntese por favor abajo.*"

"Ah, thank you…I guess," Rob said, taking the seat.

"*Bien.*" She laughed and spooned heaping amounts of beans, rice, and eggs mixed with meat and cactus onto a plate. "*Nopales,*" she said, sliding the plate in front of Rob. "Tortillas?" She held the basket and Rob grabbed two, then dropped them back into the basket, wondering how she had handled the pieces of bread over the open flame, when they still scorched his fingers. He quickly fished them out of the basket and dropped them on the plate as she giggled.

"Thanks," he said as she filled a cup with coffee. He took a bite of the eggs and paused as the blended flavors attacked his taste buds.

"*Bien?*" She was staring at him with dark eyes from across the table.

"My Lord, this is delicious!"

"*Bien,*" she said with a laugh as he shoveled the food into his mouth. She refilled his plate and he ate slower this time, talking as she took dainty bites and answered his questions in broken English. He learned she had been married once, but her husband had died at the hands of the

Comanches, during one of the attacks on the village. He also learned Teresa Romero had no children, and was *años de veinte siete viejos*, or twenty seven years old…if he understood right. The one thing Rob was certain of, was that Teresa Romero was the prettiest and nicest woman he had ever talked to. He hated to leave, and spent the entire afternoon following her around and helping with chores. Finally, when he could find no further excuse, he asked how much he owed for the meal.

"*No es importante, Señor,*" she said with a shrug. Rob laid more than enough money on the table and excused himself. He noticed her smile had vanished for the first time as he went out the door.

Billy was still involved in his poker game, and guessing by the pile of chips stacked in front of him, was doing fairly well. Rob had little interest in watching a game of poker, so he chose to wander the streets of Carrizo Springs awhile longer, until he once again found himself in front of Teresa Romero's *jacale*. It was getting dark, and she was again bent over the adobe stove, heating an evening meal for her and her grandmother.

"*Hola, Señor Roberto.* Do you wish to join us?" She flashed him a big smile.

"Yes, Ma'am."

"Come, *por favor.*" She again motioned with her head as she entered the door.

Yes, ma'am, you'll never know how much I'd like to join you. He followed her inside and closed the door.

After they had finished eating, Rob helped clean the dishes and sat listening as Teresa played a guitar and sang. He thought she had a lovely voice, and was sorry when she set the guitar in the corner to check on her grandmother.

"Well, Ma'am, I reckon I'd better be seeing if there isn't a hotel or someplace to sleep in this town."

"You have no place to stay?" She stared at him a

minute before kissing her grandmother on the head and covering her with a thin blanket.

"No, Ma'am," he said with a chuckle. "My brother's got himself hooked into a card game at the saloon, and I've been having so much fun being here with you, I haven't looked for a place."

Teresa stood at the open window for a long minute before staring up into his face with watery eyes.

"*Usted puede pasar la noche aqua. Tengo una cama additional.*"

"I beg your pardon?"

"I say you may spend the night here…with me, if you wish. I have an extra bed." She pointed toward a small cot lining the opposite wall.

"And where will you sleep?"

"I will lay with my grandmother."

"Are you sure?"

"*Si.*" She grabbed his saddlebags from where he had draped them across a chair, and laid them on the cot. "You may wash in the *baño*, out back." She took him by the hand and led him through the back door to a galvanized tub inside a lean-to attached to the house, with a plank floor. "I will heat *agua*." She was gone before Rob could reply.

Since this was better than wandering the streets looking for a place to stay, or having to watch his brother gamble, Rob retrieved his bags and waited for Teresa to return with the water.

He bathed and changed into clean clothes, then sat on the edge of the cot wondering what he should sleep in, considering he was rooming with two women. Finally deciding to sleep in his long johns, he unbuttoned his pants as he listened to Teresa singing while she bathed in the same tub he had been in earlier. He paused with the trousers around his ankles, wondering if she had changed the water, but quickly tossed the pants aside and covered himself when the singing stopped. She came in, dressed in a cotton nightgown, and stood by the lamp, brushing her hair.

"*Buonas noches, Señor.*"

"Good night, Teresa." Rob could see her form through the thin gown as she stood in front of the lamp. It was as perfect as her face, and he was sorry when she blew the lamp out. He had no idea when he had fallen asleep, but her breath against his ear woke him.

"*Hola, mi amor.*"

His heart pounded wildly as she slipped into the cot beside him. The nightgown was gone. Teresa Romero didn't bite, and had no wonderland like Alice, but she was warm and passionate. She might have been eleven years his senior, but Rob Mayfield knew he could love this woman...perhaps even more than Clara Jean...if that were possible. It took every ounce of strength he could muster to tell her about Clara.

"*Gracias,*" she said, kissing him lightly on the lips when he finished. "I am glad to know about her." Then, wrapping her arms around him, she nuzzled her head against his chest and fell asleep. He woke the next morning to her singing and the smell of fresh tortillas.

Chapter 44

"There you are. Someone told me I'd find you here. Rob was busy stoking a fire in the adobe stove when Billy unlatched the gate and strode into the yard.

"Morning, Bill. Finish your game?" Rob tossed a few more sticks into the stove as the flames caught.

"Which one? I've played several games since I last saw you. That was three days ago, little brother. I took a room at the hotel, and I've been looking all over for you. What are you doing, working here for room and board?"

"Something like that. Did you do okay?"

"Yeah, I did real good. No need for you to..." He trailed off as Teresa's voice drifted through the open door.

"Robo, se enciende el fuego?"

Rob glared at his brother before answering. *"Si,* the fire is lit."

"What the..." Billy started with a laugh, but stared in silence as Teresa came through the door carrying a frying pan in one hand, and a bowl tucked neatly in her other arm.

"Better close your mouth, big brother, before you get a fly in it. And, to answer your question before you ask it, yes, she's a nice woman and my friend, so hands off." Rob took the bowl from Teresa and kissed her lightly on the cheek.

"Roberto," she said, and swatted him playfully, "not in front of company." She slid the pan onto the grate and took Billy in with one quick look from the black hat, to his shiny boots. "And who is your friend you are talking to, *mi*

amour?"

"This is the brother I told you about, Billy. Bill," Rob slipped an arm around Teresa's shoulder with pride, "meet Teresa."

"*Amperio hora, asi que usted est'a el Billy, mi hermano mayor de Roberto's? Bien, Buena mañana, Billy.*" Teresa grabbed Billy's hand and gave him a quick kiss on the cheek, then turned just as quickly to give Rob a hug and kiss on the mouth.

"It is so good your brother has come to visit. I will make more *nopales. Una momento.*" She dashed back into the house, leaving Rob holding the bowl of raw scrambled eggs.

"My hell, little brother," Billy said with a laugh. "Here I was thinking I was a big winner 'cause I won a few dollars. Looks like you hit the jackpot. Is she for real?"

"Yeah, she's for real."

"And this is where you've been for the past three days?"

"Yeah, right here. I can't understand everything she says, especially when she talks fast like that, but I like her…I like her a lot, Billy. And I think she kind of likes me too."

"Oh, she likes you alright, idgit." Billy punched Rob on the shoulder, causing some of the egg mixture to splash over the rim of the bowl. "And whadda ya mean, you *think* she likes you? Didn't you two…?" He trailed off as Teresa appeared in the doorway, but disappeared back inside just a quickly.

"Yeah, we sleep in the same cot, if that's what you mean."

"Pardon me," Teresa said as reappeared through the doorway. "I forget the cactus." She tossed the contents into the heated pan, then cracked several more eggs and began stirring. "And what were you men discussing while I was gone?"

"I was telling my brother what a great cook you are," Rob said.

"Oh," Teresa smiled, then caressed and kissed his cheek, "you are a sweet boy, and I will teach you too, *mi amor*."

******

It was while they were finishing breakfast, that Billy broke the news they were leaving. "It'll only be for a couple of days, I promise," he said holding his right hand high as Teresa dropped her fork. Her eyes watered as he continued, causing a tear to spill over. "Three at the most, then I'll send him back to you. Honest."

"And why must you go to this place?" She shoved her plate aside and gripped Rob's hand tightly.

"A man I used to work for owes me a lot of money, and I had to wait until he sold his cattle. He should have the money by now, but there's a lot of cut-throats and thieves out there, and I didn't want to be carrying that much cash around by myself."

"And what will you do with that money, once you have it? You, you can't just keep it with you. Someone will steal it," she said, shaking her head.

"I reckon you're right. I plan on putting it in the bank at San Antonio, then you can have Rob back…I promise. Hell, I might even stay here in Carrizo Springs myself…that is, if you have a friend or sister that looks anything like you."

Yeah, I just might do that, Billy thought as he watched Rob and Teresa across the table. *Land's cheap enough. I could buy me a good-sized spread with the money Lester owes me, and add onto it little by little, and build a kingdom right here in Carrizo Springs. Wouldn't that get that old bastard's goat? Me having a ranch twenty miles north of his?*

Chapter 45

Teresa Romero wiped a tear from her cheek and spooned warm broth into her grandmother's mouth. She had helped Rob pack, then wrapped a midday meal of tortillas, chilies and meat in oilcloth for them to take, then said goodbye. She had not planned on becoming attached to someone so young, but she had been desperately lonely since Refugio died, and Rob's presence had filled that void. At first, it was simply his being there...someone to talk to. He was shy and polite, and not after her body like the men in town. She had made that mistake once, several months earlier, when she allowed the owner of the cantina to visit. After gorging himself on her food and drinking tequila, the smelly man pawed at her body, then forced himself on her when she refused. He crowned his cruelty by bragging about their encounter, and a steady line of smelly, drunken men began hounding her day and night. Teresa had finally stopped them by shooting at several with Refugio's pistol. But Rob Mayfield had been different. She sensed the hurt he was carrying, and knew he was also lonely. They were like two wounded souls coming together and becoming one.

That first night had not been planned, but lying on the cot beside her ailing grandmother, Teresa felt as if she were withering like the old woman next to her. Her grandmother's mind had quit working long ago, even before Refugio's death. Grandmother had been someone for Teresa to care for, but was not capable of offering love and comfort in return. Teresa watched Rob sleeping from across the room well into the night, remembering what it was like to sleep with a man, to have his arms around her, loving and protecting her. She had removed the nightgown and crossed the room, before realizing what she was doing, then stood in the trickle of moonlight that seeped through the opened window, watching him. Then finally, when the loneliness became unbearable, Teresa Romero slipped onto the cot next to Rob and kissed his cheek. The boy responded, but not like she had expected. He did not paw or hurt her like the owner of the cantina, but moved slowly and held her tenderly as he told her about the girl he had promised to marry. When he had finished, Rob held her close, caressing her. Then, they slept...the first real sleep she had had since Refugio's death.

While their relationship had not been a sexual one, she considered it love-making in the truest sense. They spent three days laughing, working and teasing each other. She had fallen in love with a boy. No, that wasn't right, she thought. Rob Mayfield was a man trapped inside a boy's body, and now he was gone and the loneliness returned. His brother swore he would send him back, and Rob promised to return, but she was not sure.

Teresa Romero kissed her grandmother's forehead and placed the empty bowl on the table, then wiped another tear from her cheek with resolve. She would not let this happen to her a second time. She would go to the church and pray to the Virgin Mother, asking her to make him return. If the Holy Mother would do this, she would make him love her and forget about the girl on the farm. They would be married in the church by her priest and she would never allow him to leave her again. Teresa was a better cook than the cruel man at the cantina, and had been thinking for some time of opening a restaurant of her own. She mentioned this to Rob while they were making *empanadas*, and found him eager to help her. They began making plans and estimating what such an adventure might cost. He was young, strong and trustworthy, and eager to learn. She would teach him to cook, and he could take over the duties when they had children. She knew there might be those who would laugh and jeer at her for choosing such a young husband, but let them. Teresa Romero knew Rob Mayfield was right for her, and she vowed to never be lonely again.

Chapter 46

Albert Lippert sat at the table and took his time pouring a mug from the pitcher and proceeded to take a long swallow of Mexican beer. It was cool inside the small cantina at Carrizo Springs and his skin still stung from sweat, alkali dust and the sun's heat. The cool beer trickling down his parched throat seemed to make the world okay once again.

"They ain't here," he said, eyeing his brothers across the table.

"Well, that ain't exactly earth-shaking news, is it? I got that much from the bartender when he brung the beer," Vernon growled. "What I want to know is where'n the hell they're at?"

"I'm coming to that," Albert said, swallowing some more beer.

"We're waiting." Vernon glared.

"Feller at the livery said they headed toward Cool Water just this morning. He said it's only some twenty miles or so down the road. We'd more'n likely catch up with 'em if we left right now."

"Na," Vernon said, slowly shaking his head. "We're tuckered out and the horses are even worser. No sense in facing Billy until we got our senses about us. I wanna do this right. We've waited this long, one more day won't make no nevermind." He leaned back in his chair and grinned, showing the several gaps from missing teeth.

"I'll tell you what we're gonna do. We're gonna sit right here and drink five or six more pitchers and put on the feedbag. Then we'll get ourselves some shuteye, and might even have time for a woman. Then, after we're rested, we'll leave outa here before sunup and take care of our friend Billy."

Chapter 47

Rob stopped his horse and stared in disbelief. Cool Water, Texas couldn't be called a town by any stretch of imagination. In fact, it wasn't a town at all, but consisted of a few houses and *jacales* scattered haphazardly on the Texas plain, with one small general store, a combination blacksmith and livery stable, a fair-sized saloon and dance hall, one small bank and an even smaller church. The name *Cool Water* had been taken form Lester Bishop's ranch, *Cool Water Cattle Ranch.* Lester had discovered the natural springs while buying cattle in Piedrao Negras, Mexico and promptly bought the land, one-thousand acres of it, and built his ranch.

After having a heated argument with some bankers in San Antonio, Lester decided to build his own city, and plans were drawn, subdividing the town-site. He next began negotiating with the International Great-Northern railroad to build a spur to his ranch. Believing middle management personnel were beneath him, Lester went to Chicago and finagled a meeting with the chairman of the board. The man listened politely, then promptly refused him, saying San Antonio already had three railroads, and two others scheduled for the near future.

"Building a spur to your ranch doesn't make financial sense, Mr. Bishop. We would only be hauling cattle from your ranch, and perhaps small amounts of goods from Carrizo Springs, if we chose to build a depot there…which is not likely. Besides, it's only what, sixty or seventy miles from your ranch to San Antonio? Seventy, or even a hundred miles isn't much of a cattle drive for a Texan."

"Look," he said when Lester began to argue, "build your town, and if you can prove there would be enough profit...enough passengers, cattle and goods to make it feasible...I'll personally push the idea."

The idea never took hold, no matter how much effort and money Lester Bishop invested. Marauding Indians and bandits plagued the area, killing settlers, and making off with his cattle. Five years and thousands of dollars later, Cool Water, Texas was not even a recognized town-site, other than in Lester Bishop's mind. His four successes, which he gloried in, were the store, where the people living on his ranch and the surrounding area bought goods at inflated prices; the saloon and dance hall, where his cowboys spent their hard-earned money on cheap liquor and even cheaper whores who gave Lester a cut of their profits; his granddaughter, Ruth, who he thought was the loveliest girl in Texas and who he thought no one of a lesser social status than himself worthy of marrying; and his bank, but not necessarily in that order. If the truth were known, the bank was his crowning achievement, since it had never been robbed, and kept his ever growing stash of money safe and sound.

"You've got to be joking," Rob said, as he sat on his horse in the middle of the nonexistent main street. "We spent two months, and rode five hundred miles for this?"

"Sure isn't much is it?" Billy grinned at his brother, causing him to get even angrier.

"You made me leave Clara Jean and Teresa Romero for this? What in the Sam-hill is the matter with you?"

"Nothing, little brother. Like I said, Lester Bishop owns this town, and he owes me five thousand dollars."

"Five thousand?" Rob almost yelled the number.

"Yes, five thousand. I checked the price of beeves

when we were in San Antonio, and they are selling at twenty-five dollars a head. You were good in school, you do the ciphering. Six hundred head at twenty five dollars each, comes to fifteen thousand. My cut is five thousand." Billy nudged his horse in the direction of the saloon.

"Like I said, I'm not greedy. I plan on giving you half."

"Half of your five thousand?"

"Uh-huh," Billy said as he dismounted. "Think what you can do with twenty-five hundred in your pocket, little brother. You and that Mexican gal could build a real nice restaurant with that kind of money. Or, you could go back to Clara Jean, and buy your own farm. Or, if you didn't like either of those ideas, you could come to New Orleans with me. It's up to you. Come on," he added as Rob continued staring opened-mouthed, "I'll buy you a beer."

Chapter 48

"What are you doing here, Billy?" Rob got the feeling he and his brother were not exactly welcome in Cool Water, not only by the sound of the bartender's voice, but by the stares they were getting from the handful of cowboys inside the saloon. One of the scantily-clad girls started their way, but another stopped her by grabbing her arm and whispering in her ear.

"I wanted to buy my brother a beer, Charlie. You got a problem with that?" Billy tossed the money on the bar and leaned against the counter with an almost too-wide grin.

"No, I just don't want any trouble, Billy." The bartender filled two mugs with room-temperature beer. "You know you aren't welcome around here." He slid the mugs on the counter.

Rob tasted the beer and set the mug back on the counter. It tasted sour.

"Me, not welcome? Na...I can't believe that," Billy said with a laugh. He leaned with his back against the counter and surveyed the saloon's interior. "Place hasn't changed a bit, has it?"

"No, and you haven't either. Now, you two'd better finish your beers and get out of here," the bartender said, vigorously wiping the counter with a dirty towel. "Mr. Bishop will be arriving any minute."

"Yeah, I know. That's why I'm here." Billy toasted the bartender with his mug, and turned toward Rob.

"You see, little brother, Ol' Lester comes in here

around eleven every morning, to get his cut from whatever Charlie and the girls made the night before. Ain't that right, Ladies?" He toasted the girls at the opposite end of the bar.

"Then he does the same at the store and the blacksmith shop, and takes the money over and deposits it in his bank. And ol' Lester's prompt. You can set your watch by him coming in here every day, except on Sundays. Lester won't enter the saloon on Sunday, no sir. That's when the old hypocrite goes to church and sings hymns and prays. He might even put a little of the money he took from these girls in the offering plate." He hoisted the mug high and raised his voice.

"Here's to Lester Bishop, king of Cool Water, Texas!"

The door swung open and two young cowboys came in laughing, but stopped at the sight of Billy.

"Billy," one of them said, "what the hell are you doing here?"

"I've been asked that twice since we walked in here. I'm beginning to think Cool Water is a mighty unfriendly town."

"It is, for you."

"Aw, come on, I'm not after trouble. Here, I'll buy you boys a beer." Billy tossed more money on the counter. "Give Dusty and Utah a couple of beers, Charlie."

"Thanks for the beer, Billy, but you'd better finish and get going," the one called Dusty said.

"Na-uh," Billy said, shaking his head. "You know me better'n that, Dusty. That old skinflint owes me a ton of money. You sat at that table in the corner last spring, and watched him lose the entire herd. Now, I know he's sold his cattle, and I'm here to collect."

"He won't give it to you," Utah said. "He got market price, and he won't part with that kind of money without a fight."

"I'm not looking for a fight. In fact, I'm not asking for the entire amount. I just want a third, simply on principle." Billy slammed his mug on the counter as a tall, thin man with gray hair and a hard, weathered look entered. He was followed by two more cowboys. Both looked as hard as the old man.

"What the hell are you doing here? Get out," the old man ordered.

"My, my, I do believe Cool Water is the unfriendliest town I've been in," Billy said, and shook his head.

"I said, get out," the man shouted and pointed toward the door.

"Not until I've got my money."

"What money? I don't owe you a penny." Lester Bishop grew red in the face. The two hard-looking cowboys casually moved to opposite sides of the bar, keeping Rob and Billy in the middle. Beads of sweat popped out on Rob's brow as Utah and Dusty grabbed the two scantily-clad girls and huddled in a far corner of the saloon.

"Sure you do. Remember? The money you got for selling my cattle."

"What cattle? You never owned a cow in your life, and I wouldn't allow it on my ranch if you did."

"You know, Lester, it isn't right for a Christian to lie like that. You lost the eastern herd, all six-hundred head, in a poker game, right over at that table." Billy pointed. "Now, I know you sold them for market price, but I'm not asking for the entire fifteen thousand, because I'm not greedy and know you have to pay the boys. But I *do* want a third, just on principle." Lester Bishop burst out laughing. "Me…give you five thousand dollars? After what you've done? Get the hell off my ranch before I have Curley and Westfall kill you."

"New boys of yours," Billy said, and glanced at the men standing at opposite ends of the bar.

"Yes, and don't even think of trying to match them.

You wouldn't stand a chance. Now, take your friend and get off my ranch before I lose patience."

"Okie-dokie, I'm leaving." Billy downed the remaining beer in one gulp and grinned. "I just thought you might be a man of his word…but I guess not."

"You're pushing me, Mayfield."

"Don't have a stroke, we're leaving," Billy said, raising a hand. He paused at the door and looked back.

"Mind if I buy a couple of things at the store?"

"Stay the hell out of my store!"

"I thought so." Billy laughed, and Rob followed him through the door.

Chapter 49

"You've gotta be kidding." Rob Mayfield crinkled his brow and glared across the campfire at his brother, then added, "You are, aren't you," when Billy grinned back at him. They were camped in a clump of brush and mesquite near a creek, approximately a half a mile outside the Cool Water Ranch. "I hope you *are* kidding, 'cause I don't like it."

"What's not to like? It's a snap job. In and out. Boom, boom, just like that."

"Because it's robbing a bank, that's what's not to like," Rob yelled. "And, if it's so easy, what do you need me for? Why don't you just walk in there and grab it all for yourself?"

"Well, I just might do that." Billy shot Rob a look of disgust. "I'm starting to wonder why I even brought you along. The only reason I can think of is, 'cause you're the only family I've got. But don't push it."

"People go to prison or get killed robbing banks, Bill. Besides, we've got a couple hundred dollars between us right now. Why do we need to rob a bank? We could make it to New Orleans on what we've got."

"You know how far two hundred dollars is going to get us? Not very damn far, I'll tell you that. We might make it to New Orleans, but we wouldn't have much when we got there. Besides, it's the principle of the thing. I'm not going to let that old bastard get away with cheating me out of five thousand dollars. In fact, I might take the whole fifteen thousand for good measure." Billy tossed the remnants of his coffee and refilled his cup as he continued. "It should be quick and easy, and I don't want to pass the opportunity to teach Lester Bishop a lesson."

Rob shook his head as Billy began wiping his shiny black boots with a cloth. *No one's gonna care what your boots look like while they're shoveling dirt in your face.*

"Look," Billy heaved a deep sigh, "we're only about twenty miles or so from the Mexican border. We've got a straight run if something did go wrong," he pointed south, "but nothing is. We hit the bank hard and fast as soon as it opens. We'll have five miles on Lester and his gun-hands before they know what happened."

"And what's gonna stop Lester's cowhands from crossing the border? They ain't lawmen, Billy. Think about it some." Rob tossed another stick into the fire and trudged off toward the stream. It wasn't more than a trickle, and if the drought lasted much longer, it would dry up completely.

"Okay," Billy raised his voice. "We'll both think on it. I'll wait for your answer, but if you don't want in, don't get in my way. 'Cause I'm going with or without you."

"Yeah, I know you will." Rob flung a stone at the trickle in the streambed, and sat wishing his brother would forget the whole idea. He'd never so much as stolen a stick of candy from *Whitefield's General Store* when he was a kid growing up in Bishop, and here was Billy asking him to steal a bank-full of money. How much money could that little bank have in it anyway? He knew Billy claimed it was loaded, but Rob wasn't too sure. The town wasn't even a town. He had only counted ten, maybe twenty people, including Lester Bishop, while in Cool Water. There were probably no more than a couple hundred people in a five or six mile radius, unless you counted the Mexican bandits and Comanche Indians, and they wouldn't deposit anything in a bank. If he were smart, he would pack his gear and cut out on his own and let Billy do what he wanted. He could be at Teresa's tomorrow afternoon, then head toward Pittsburg and Clara Jean the following day. He flung another stone in disgust. The fact was, he felt he owed his brother something. No one had forced Billy to return home for him after Ma died. Billy had been on his own for several years when that happened, and it would have been easy for him to have stayed that way. Instead, he had returned home, and had been looking out for him in one fashion or the other ever since.

Rob flung another stone as he walked back to the campfire and found Billy dressing the rabbit they had snared earlier. Rob took the coffeepot to the stream and filled it without speaking. He added the grounds and placed the pot on a rock at the edge of the fire and heaved a sigh.

"Okay, Billy," he glared across the fire, "I'll think about it and let you know in the morning. But if I go with you, we're done. I'm pulling out and heading to Carrizo Springs. You can go to New Orleans by yourself."

"Alright," Billy nodded, "But I wouldn't be stopping in Carrizo Springs, even if you don't go with me. It's only twenty miles or so from Cool Water, and folks in both places have seen us together. Someone's bound to recognize you, and think you were in on this deal. I'd head toward Mexico and send for that Teresa Romero girl. You two could open the restaurant you were talking about, especially with two thousand dollars. That's if you help me with the bank. If not, I'd still recommend heading toward Mexico, then work your way back to that skinny farm girl with the two hundred we've already got.

"Now," Billy poked a stick through the rabbit and held it over the fire, "let's work on getting this rabbit and coffee done. I'm hungry."

The cottontail wasn't half-bad in Rob's opinion, and the coffee was even better. Rob sipped a second cup as Billy brought the finish on his boot to a high gloss. He discussed the plans for robbing the bank in detail as he worked and Rob listened.

"Okay, if you come with me, this is how we'll do it. We hit the bank as soon as it opens at ten. Lester and the two hired guns won't be arriving from the ranch house until eleven. Lester's house is almost a mile west of town, and it'll take someone a few minutes to let him know what's happened. Then, Lester will have to get ready and head into town...that'll take him another ten minutes or so. Then, even with the hired guns, he'll want to form some sort of posse, 'cause that's the way Lester thinks. The way I figure, we'll have ourselves a good fifteen, maybe twenty minute jump. Our horses are rested, and it's a straight shot to Mexico. We'll be drinking tequila and dancing with dark-eyed girls before they know what hit 'em."

Rob was about to ask what his brother planned to do if there was any shooting, when some movement in the bushes caught his eye. "Hey, Billy," he said spilling his coffee. "There's something out there."

"Huh? Where?" Billy dropped the shine-rag and grabbed one of the pearl-handled pistols.

"Over there...by that clump of mesquites near the creek."

"Okay, I see it. You start over there to the right," Billy motioned with his gun, "and I'll go up over here. And take your gun out its holster, for Christ's sake," he added as Rob started creeping forward. They searched behind every tree, bush and rock, but came up empty-handed, until they spied the goat nibbling at mesquite berries downstream.

"Hell, if I'd known you were running loose, I would have roasted you instead of the cottontail," Billy said, holstering his gun. "The Mexican ranchers around here all run goat herds, and I guess this one got away, and that's what you saw. Come on, let's get some more coffee."

"Maybe," Rob stared at the .44 caliber Smith and

Wesson in his hand before dropping it back into the holster, "but I ain't so sure."

"We didn't find anything but the goat, did we?"

Rob shook his head.

"You go check on the horses, if you're so uneasy, and then hit the hay. We've got ourselves a big day tomorrow."

Rob nodded and went to where the horses were tied. He could see Billy sitting by the fire, smoking, as he gave his mustang a rubdown, wondering how his brother could be so relaxed after making plans to rob a bank. It caused him to wonder what other deeds Billy had done while he was away. Rob waited until Billy had rolled himself in his blankets, before bedding down next to the fire. But try as he might, Rob Mayfield could not sleep, and spent the night staring at the stars, wondering what was happening to him and where it might lead.

All he'd ever wanted was to be a farmer like his father. He kept wishing he had stayed in Douglass, or with Clara Jean. Perhaps he should saddle his horse and leave while it was still dark, and return to Carrizo Springs and help Teresa open her restaurant. It wasn't until Billy crawled out of his blankets and began stoking the fire that Rob knew what he was going to do.

Chapter 50

They shared a breakfast of coffee and bacon, then broke camp. Billy was about to mount his horse when Rob stopped him.

"I made up my mind, Bill, and we ain't going."

"Well, I kinda figured you might be chickening out on me, by the way you showed yellow last night. So, you can just get on your horse and head wherever you want. I'll get the money Lester owes me."

"Na-uh. You're not going either." Rob drew and leveled his gun at him.

"So, that's the way it is, is it, little brother?" Billy snickered as he let go of the saddle and turned to face Rob.

"Yeah, that's the way it is. We're gonna get on our horses and head outta here. And once we're clear of Carrizo Springs, you're on your own. I don't care what you do, as long as you leave me out of it."

"Well now, that's just fine." Billy placed his hands on his hips and grinned. "My little brother's finally showing some spine. But, let me ask you one question."

"What's that?"

"Why wait until we ride all the way to Carrizo Springs? Why not end our association right here and now?"

Rob thought his head had exploded as Billy slapped the gun away and slammed his pearl-handled pistol against his head. He woke several minutes later to find his brother mounted and staring at him. He had unbuckled Rob's gunbelt and hooked it around the saddle horn, and was holding the reins to Rob's horse in his left hand.

"You're getting off easy. I would have killed anyone else pulling down on me the way you did. The only reason I didn't bore you was, you're my brother. But don't try something like that again. And you'd better be willing to shoot if you decide to pull on anyone in the future, 'cause they'll blow your brains out, quicker'n you can spit.

"I'll leave your horse and gun a couple of miles north of here in the brush. I'd keep heading north, if I were you, 'cause I'll be finished in Cool Water long before you find it."

Rob watched as his brother led his horse away and disappeared through the brush. Holding a handkerchief to his wounded cheek, Rob stumbled forward, following the tracks left by the horses. Sweat began to sting his wounded cheekbone, and he paused to stare at the sun. It was going to be a hot one, without a cloud showing in the sky. His throat already felt parched, and he wished he had his canteen. It wasn't a good day for the cotton farmers either, he thought, and continued staggering forward, wondering how he had gotten himself into such a mess.

Chapter 51

The street was deserted when Billy tied his horse in front of the bank exactly five minutes after ten. There was only one horse in front of the general store, and another in front of the livery, but no people. Billy pulled two empty flour sacks from his saddle bags and entered the bank.

The teller was a young man with thick glasses who moved with a nervous twitch and talked at a rabbit's pace. He was finishing with a heavyset woman with a red face when Billy took his place in line. The only other customer was a Mexican rancher. A fat man with graying hair and a frown sat behind a desk in the corner. A sign carved into a block of wood set on the edge of the desk read, *Manager.*

Billy waited until the fat woman left, then calmly crowded behind the Mexican and pointed a gun at the teller. "Okay, gentlemen, it's time to make a big withdrawal. Up with the hands, and be quick about it."

"You can't do this, Billy! Mr. Bishop will hunt you down like a dog." The manager scooted his chair away from the desk and stood up.

"Get your fat butt back into that chair." Billy swung the gun in the manager's direction, and the manager dropped to the chair. The chair tipped, breaking one of the arms as it hit the floor. "You move again, and you're dead." He motioned toward the teller with his head. "Let's get the bags filled."

"How much?" The teller pissed his pants as he shoved stacks of bills into a bag with trembling hands.

"All of it."

"All?"

"You heard me, everything but the coin...even what's in the safe. It's open. I can see it from here."

******

Marshall Clay Best leaned just inside the doorway of the general store smoking his pipe and watching the bank. He had received a tip the bank might be robbed, and even knew who was going to commit the robbery. He had been expecting two bandits and was surprised when only one man showed. He quickly surveyed the dusty roadway, then shrugged toward the two deputies he had posted inside the blacksmith shop. He motioned them toward the bank, but quickly waved them back as three riders galloped into view. The men tied their horses in front of the saloon and walked toward the bank, where one of them checked the saddle and bags on the lone bandit's tan mustang and nodded. The men then checked their guns and posted themselves facing the bank door.

"Dammit!" Clay knocked the ashes from his pipe and checked the loads in his own gun. He recognized the men from a description on a wanted poster he had picked up in San Antonio two days earlier. They were killers and were after the man inside the bank. What Clay had hoped would be a peaceful ending to a simple robbery had turned deadly. He motioned his men into position as the bank door flew open.

******

With the bags filled, Billy backed toward the door, still covering the people inside the bank. Everything was going as planned, until he reached the sidewalk and a loud voice turned his blood cold.

"Alright gambler, turn around and get yours!"

Billy could see one of the men from the corner of his eye. He didn't know the man, but he had a gun pointed at him. The gun in Billy's left hand roared as he swung and pulled the trigger. The man went down but Billy was propelled against the bank wall as the street erupted in gunfire. He staggered forward and flopped like a rag doll, lying partly on the sidewalk, and partly in the dirty street.

The gunfire ceased and Billy felt as though a huge weight was pressing against his chest. He couldn't have moved if he wanted to. The light was beginning to fade as a large man with a badge and droopy mustache knelt beside him. Billy could see genuine concern on his face.

"I'm Marshall Clay Best, and I'm sorry it had to end this way."

"Jessie's dead, Marshall." One of the men looked up from the fallen deputy.

"Hell," the Marshall said. "He has two kids and a wife. Now, I'm gonna have to tell her that her husband's dead. Dammit! Take this man over to the doc's and see if he can't do something for him."

Billy glanced at his boots as several men hoisted him in their arms. They were dusty. Then the light quickly vanished, leaving him in darkness.

Chapter 52

Rob found his horse tied to a clump of brush next to a trickle of water in a creek bed. He washed the dried blood from his face and drank from the stream before untying the horse. The water tasted salty. He turned the horse north and had almost reached Carrizo Springs before stopping and staring back over his shoulder.

"Aw hell, Billy," he said, and turned his horse around.

The sun was hanging low in the sky when he walked the lathered animal into Cool Water. Outside of the cluster of horses tied in front of the saloon, the town almost looked deserted. He was exhausted, and his skin felt as dry as the dust clinging to his clothes. A dusty haze hung in the air, stinging his eyes and filling his nostrils with the salty tinge of alkali. A man in front of the store with a white apron stopped sweeping to point and say something to a woman as he passed.

"Excuse me!" Rob glanced over his shoulder to see the woman wave a handkerchief as she chased after him in the dusty street. "Please excuse me," she repeated. Rob reigned to a halt and waited.

"I'm sorry to bother you," she said, laying a gloved hand against his arm. "Harold Thomas said you are Billy Mayfield's brother. Is that true?"

"Yes Ma'am."

"Then, maybe you should come with me."

"Why, Ma'am?"

"Because...," she hesitated, "something terrible's happened, and I think you need to talk to my husband."

"I don't know you or your husband. I don't even know who Harold Thomas is, or anyone else in this town."

"Oh, I'm sorry. I'm June Best, and my husband Clay is the town marshal. I think you really need to talk to him."

"Billy?" Rob didn't need her nod to confirm his feeling. "Lord have mercy," he said, sliding from the saddle. He followed the small, frail-looking woman toward a house sitting at the edge of town as a dog barked somewhere in the distance.

Chapter 53

"Mind if I smoke my pipe?"

Rob shook his head, and the Marshall began packing the pipe with tobacco. June Best had cleaned and doctored Rob's battered face before starting to prepare supper. The men were presently sitting on the front porch, listening to the loud voices and the out-of-key piano coming from inside the saloon. Up to this point, neither man had been willing to discuss the events of the day.

"Reckon you want to know what come off this morning," Marshall Best finally said. He blew a cloud of smoke into the air and eyed Rob through the haze.

"I've got an idea," Rob said with a nod. "Are you the one who killed him?"

"Billy? No." He shook his head and took another draw on the pipe. "It was the Lipperts who shot your brother."

"Lipperts? Who are the Lipperts, and why would they want to kill Billy? We don't know any Lipperts."

"No? Well they sure knew you boys. They would've more'n likely killed you, if you had been here."

"Why?" Rob shook his head, staring at the weathered planking beneath his feet.

"Seems your brother killed their older brother Harry over a card game, and they were out for revenge. Those boys were meaner'n a wounded Comanche and left a string of dead and busted-up folks clean across Texas looking for you two. I knew what your brother was up to and had deputized me a couple of Billy's friends, thinking he might be willing to give himself up if he was facing them."

"You knew? How?" Rob turned his attention toward the man smoking the pipe.

"Well, that was a case of pure accident. Harley Wright's got a twelve-year-old boy who's pet goat keeps getting out of his pen. He was out looking for him when he overheard y'all discussing robbing the bank. Then, he did the right thing and told me. I didn't want none of it to happen, I want you to know that, son." Marshall Best took an angry puff from his pipe and continued.

"Like I said, I deputized a couple of Billy's friends, and we'd planned on talking him into giving hisself up. Then, I'd planned on carting him over to Austin where I know Judge Keller personally. I figured he'd more than likely give him a few months in jail and a swift kick in the britches before sending him on his way. But the Lipperts showed up and all hell broke loose. Billy killed one of them, and the other two did for your brother before I could kill them."

They sat in silence a couple of minutes as the smell of frying potatoes, onions and bacon floated through the window.

"Billy said Lester Bishop owed him a lot of money," Rob said absently.

"I reckon he did. I told Lester I thought he was giving your brother a raw deal, but that don't help none. Robbing a bank ain't no way of settling a debt. Your brother's dead and out his money. You're without your brother and ol' skinflint Lester's the winner no matter how you deal the cards. No, sir. Your brother knew Lester was after his hide over that granddaughter of his, and wasn't gonna give him a plug nickel, no matter how much money he won at the table. Even if he took him to court, none of the punchers in that room would have told the truth, because they'd lose their job.

Besides, ol' Lester hand-picked the local judge, same as he picked me."

"You're in Lester Bishop's pocket?" Rob twisted in his chair to glare.

"Me?" Clay Best snorted. "Na, that old bastard didn't know what he was getting when he got me. He knew my record as a lawman, and wanted someone to track down rustlers and whatnot. We've locked horns more'n once since my coming here.

"No, sir. June's the reason I'm here, you know?" He continued, although Rob didn't answer.

"She's a sick woman, son. I retired from being a real Marshall, to stay home and take care of her. We were living in San Antonio at the time, and I was gone most the time. I thought my being there might help, but she kept getting worse. A doctor said I needed to get her somewhere where the air was cleaner. He said the city was just too smoky and dirty, and she needed to be someplace like Arizona. Well, I knew June would never survive a trip like that, so it was out of the question. Then, our money started to run out, and Lester offered me the job of being City Marshall in Cool Water. The way I saw it, there wasn't much to do, and I could stay home most of the time and take care for June. Since there wasn't much of a town, the air should be clean, and you couldn't find a dryer climate. What we got was me havin' to chase bandits and Indians across the last forty acres of hell, with a lot of dust and dirt, stirred up by cattle and rowdy cowboys, and now this." He beat the ashes from his pipe against the sole of his boot. "So, you see, you and your brother ain't the only ones to make stupid mistakes. Yes, sir, I'm right up there with you.

"We've already planted the Lipperts, but were saving my deputy and your brother for the morning. Reckon you'll want to see him before then?"

"Yes sir." Rob nodded.

"He's in one of the back rooms at the saloon. Made Lester madder'n a wet hen, 'cause he's losing money from all the whore'n that goes on in there. I told him there wasn't any place else to keep bodies, since he'd failed to build a mortuary. So, in some small way, you might say your brother's getting back at him."

******

Rob ignored the food June Best had prepared and only sipped at his coffee. He had completely lost his appetite, and suspected it might never return as he stared at Billy's lifeless body. The men were lying in crudely-made wooden boxes, suspended on sawhorses next to the bed. The squeaking of rusty springs and thumping on the wall in the neighboring room told what the bed was used for. Tears trickled down June Best's cheeks as she held Rob's hand and prayed for the men lying in the coffins. Rob listened to the prayer asking Almighty God for forgiveness, and asking him to take the men into his kingdom. How ironic that it was being uttered inside a room where fornication was practiced daily.

"Where will you go now," June asked after she finished praying.

"Don't know. I've been thinking some on that question. I thought about going to Carrizo Springs and help a friend run a restaurant, but that's too close. I think I'd always be thinking about Billy and what happened here. I've been thinking about returning to Pittsburg. I know a girl whose family owns a cotton farm. I was happy there. We even talked about getting married."

"I think that would be nice," she said, squeezing his hand.

"Stop by our house before you pull out and pick up your brother's personals," the marshal said, packing his pipe. "He had some money and a few things I think he'd want you to have. Besides," he paused to fish a match from his vest pocket and light the pipe. "Seems there was a reward for the Lepperts. I'd thought about keeping it and taking June away from here, but she says she'd rather you have it. It'll take a few days to clear, but it's yours, if you want it."

"It might help you make a new start, Mister Mayfield," June said with a grin. Then, she kissed him lightly on the cheek and added, "Go marry your farm girl and stay out of trouble. In the meantime, you're welcome to stay with us."

The door opened and a young Mexican couple started to enter, but paused upon seeing them. The woman had two small bouquets of wilted prairie flowers, and the man was wearing Billy's boots.

"This is Raul and his wife," Clay said as Rob stared at the boots. "He built the coffins, and asked for the boots instead of money. Good boots are hard to come by, and I told him it was okay. Hope I didn't over-step my bounds." Rob shook his head and started to leave, but turned to look the Mexican in the eye.

"Hey, can you do me a favor?" He choked back a sob as he spoke.

"Si, what is it?"

"Wipe the dust off them boots. Billy wouldn't like it if he knew they were dirty."

"Si," he said as Rob hurried from the saloon.

End

About The Authors

MAJOR MITCHELL (pictured on the left), is the author of four historical westerns and two children's books. He lives with his wife, Judy, in Northern California. A member of The Western Writers of America and a frequent guest speaker at historical meetings and schools on the west coast, he has also written several songs, and takes the stage on rare occasions as a singer.

JERRY MITCHELL (pictured on the right), is the author of several short stories and lives with this wife, Juana, in Northern California, approximately 45 minutes from his brother Major. His ideas have been the inspiration for two of Major's novels.

For your reading pleasure, we invite you to visit our Trading Post bookstore.

http://www.books.shalakopress.com